More Praise for *Dunbar*

"[*Dunbar* is] an enjoyable, breakneck ride through the misdeeds of one of the greatest stages of fools you'll ever meet."

—*Pittsburgh Post-Gazette*

"Henry Dunbar—think Rupert Murdoch or Sumner Redstone—breaks free of an English sanatorium, set on revenge."

—*Esquire*

"A brilliant reworking of William Shakespeare's *King Lear* for our day."

—*Kirkus Reviews* (starred review)

"The tale is the perfect vehicle for what this author does best, which is to expose repellent, privileged people and their hollow dynasties in stellar prose."

—*Publishers Weekly*

Praise for Edward St. Aubyn

"Perhaps the most brilliant English novelist of his generation."

—Alan Hollinghurst

"Nothing about the plots can prepare you for the rich, acerbic comedy of St. Aubyn's world—or more surprising—its philosophical density."

—Zadie Smith, *Harper's*

"St. Aubyn conveys the chaos of emotion, the confusion of heightened sensation, and the daunting contradictions of intellectual endeavour with a force and subtlety that have an exhilarating, almost therapeutic effect."

—Francis Wyndham, *New York Review of Books*

Hogarth h Shakespeare

Dunbar

EDWARD ST. AUBYN

Hogarth Shakespeare

London   New York

Copyright © 2017 by Edward St. Aubyn

All rights reserved.
Published in the United States by Hogarth, an imprint of the Crown
Publishing Group, a division of Penguin Random House LLC, New York.
crownpublishing.com

HOGARTH is a trademark of the Random House Group Limited, and
the H colophon is a trademark of Penguin Random House LLC.

Originally published in hardcover in the United States by Hogarth,
an imprint of the Crown Publishing Group, a division of
Penguin Random House LLC, New York,
and in Great Britain by Hogarth UK,
a division of Random House Group Limited,
a Penguin Random House Company, London, in 2017.

Library of Congress Cataloging-in-Publication Data
is available upon request.

ISBN 978-1-101-90430-5
Ebook ISBN 978-1-101-90429-9

Printed in the United States of America

Cover design and illustration by Oliver Munday

10 9 8 7 6 5 4 3 2 1

First Paperback Edition

For Kate

1

"We're off our meds," whispered Dunbar.

"We're off our meds/ we're off our heads," sang Peter, "we're out of our beds/ and we're off our meds! Yesterday," he continued in a conspiratorial whisper, "we were drooling into the lapels of our terry cloth dressing gowns, but now we're off our meds! We've spat them out; we've tranquilized the aspidistras! If those fresh lilies you get sent each day . . ."

"When I think where they come from," growled Dunbar.

"Steady, old man."

"They stole my empire and now they send me stinking lilies."

"Oh, you had an empire, did you?" said Peter, in the voice of an eager hostess, "you must meet Gavin in Room 33, he's here in disguise, but his real name," Peter lowered his voice, "is *Alexander the Great*."

"I don't believe a word of it," grumbled Dunbar, "he's been dead for years."

"Well," said Peter, now a Harley Street consultant, "if those troubled lilies were suffering from schizo-phrenic tendencies; tendencies, mind you, a little pen-chant for the schizoid, not the full-blown thing, their symptoms will have been mitigated with a minimum of fatal side effects." He leant forward and whispered, "that's where I put my dead meds: in the vase with the lilies!"

"I really did have an empire, you know," said Dun-bar. "Have I ever told you the story of how it was sto-len from me?"

"Many times, old man, many times," said Peter dreamily.

Dunbar heaved himself out of his armchair and after a couple of stumbling steps, straightened up, squinting at the strong light that slanted through the reinforced glass of his premium cell.

"I told Wilson that I would stay on as non-executive chairman," Dunbar began, "keeping the plane, the entourage, the properties, and the appropriate privi-leges, but laying down the burden—" he reached over to the large vase of lilies and lowered it carefully to the floor, "laying down the burden of running the Trust from day to day. From now on, I told him, the world will be my perfect playground and, in due course, my private hospice."

"Oh, that's very good," said Peter, "'the world is my private hospice,' that's a new one."

"'But the Trust is everything,' Wilson told me." Dunbar grew more agitated as he moved into the story. "'If you give that away,' he said, 'you'll have nothing left. You can't give something away and keep it at the same time.'"

"It's an untenable position," Peter cut in, "as R. D. Laing said to the Bishop."

"Please let me tell my story," said Dunbar. "I told Wilson that it was a tax measure, that we could get around the inheritance tax by giving the girls the company straight away. 'Better pay the tax,' said Wilson, 'than disinherit yourself.'"

"Oh, I like this Wilson," said Peter. "He sounds like a sound fellow, he sounds like a man with his meds screwed on, I mean his heads screwed on."

"He only had one head," said Dunbar impatiently, "he wasn't a monster; it's my daughters who are the monsters."

"Only one head!" said Peter. "What a dull fellow! When I get anti-depressed I have more heads on my head than bees in a bonnet."

"Very well, very well," said Dunbar. He looked up at the ceiling and then boomed down in the voice of Wilson, "'You can't cling to the trappings of power, without the power itself. It's just,'" he paused, trying to avoid the word, but eventually letting it fall on him from the plaster above, "'decadent.'"

"Oh, decadence, decay, and death," said Peter in his thespian tremolo, "descending, syllable by syllable, into a narrow grave. How lightly we have tripped down those stairs, like Fred Astaires, twirling a scythe instead of a cane!"

"God in heaven," said Dunbar, his face flushing, "will you please stop interrupting me? People didn't used to interrupt me; they listened to me meekly. If they spoke, it was to flatter me, or to make lucrative insinuations. But you, you . . ."

"Okay, guys," said Peter, as if addressing an angry mob, "give the man some space. Let's hear what he's gotta say."

" 'I can do what I bloody well like!' " cried Dunbar, "that's what I told Wilson. 'I am informing you of my decision, not asking your advice. Just make it happen!' "

Dunbar raised his eyes to the ceiling again.

" 'I'm not only your lawyer, Henry; I'm your oldest surviving friend. I'm saying these things to protect you.' "

" 'You presume too much on our friendship,' I thundered. 'I will not be lectured on the company that I alone created.' " Dunbar raised his fist to the ceiling and shook it. "At that point, I seized a Fabergé egg that lay in a nest of tissue paper on my desk—it was the third one that month: how monotonous the Russians were with their imperial pretensions; bunch of jumped-up Jewish kleptocrats, pretending to be Romanov princes, I didn't need their: 'Bloody Russki trash!' I shouted, flinging the egg into the fireplace behind my desk, scattering pearls and fragments of enamel across the hearth. 'What do my daughters call it?' I asked Wilson. 'Bling! Bloody Russki bling!' "

"Wilson remained impassive; these 'infantile tantrums' had become almost daily occurrences, causing some worry to my medical team. You see," said Dunbar to Peter excitedly, "I can read his thoughts now. I've got . . ."

"I'm afraid to say that you've got psychotic insight," said Peter, the Harley Street consultant.

"Oh, pish, stop pretending to be a doctor."

"Who shall I pretend to be?" asked Peter.

"Just be yourself, for heaven's sake."

"Oh, I haven't got that one down yet, Henry. Give me someone easier to impersonate. How about John Wayne?" Peter didn't wait for an answer. "We're goin' to bust out of this joint, Henry," he drawled, "and by sundown tomorrow we'll be walkin' into the Windermere Saloon and ordering a couple of drinks from the bartender, like a couple of real men in charge of their own destinies."

"I must tell my story," wailed Dunbar. "Oh, God, let me not go mad."

"You see," said Peter, ignoring Dunbar's distress, "I am, or I was, or I used to be—who knows whether I'm history or not?—a famous comedian, but I suffer from depression, the comic affliction, or the tragic affliction of the comic, or the historic affliction of tragic comedians, or the fiction of the tragic affliction of historic comedians!"

"Please," said Dunbar, "I'm getting confused."

"Oh, I'm anti-depressed/I'm anti-depressed," sang Peter, leaping from his chair, locking arms with Dunbar and encouraging him to spin, "I'm so anti-depressed/that I'm *manic*!" He stopped suddenly and let go of Dunbar's arm. "Sound of Screeching Tyres," he cut in, in his voiceover voice, beginning to mime, "as he wrestles manfully with the steering wheel on the verge of a precipice."

"I have seen your many faces," said Dunbar vaguely, "on many screens."

"Oh, I don't claim to be unique," said Peter, with a swagger of modesty, "I'm not the only one. In fact in 1953, when I was ejected into this vale of tears by my careless mother, there were already two hundred and thirty-one Peter Walkers in the London telephone directory alone; well, not alone so much as over-crowded."

Dunbar stood frozen in the middle of the room.

"But I digress," said Peter jovially. "Tell me about your 'medical team,' old man."

"My medical team," said Dunbar, grasping at the handrail of a familiar phrase in the pitch and roll of his thoughts. "Yes, yes; only the day before I announced my decision to Wilson, Dr. Bob, my personal physician, had taken Wilson aside to tell him that I had been experiencing some 'little cerebral incidents.' He told Wilson there was 'nothing to get unduly worried about.'"

"Is there ever anything to get *unduly* worried about," Peter couldn't help asking, "when there are so many things to worry about duly?"

Dunbar waved him aside, like a man discouraging a persistent fly.

"But," Dunbar resumed, "according to the glib doctor—that gilded serpent, that dodecahedron—who should have been an expert, since his only patient was me, or I, or at any rate, myself, Henry Dunbar," he said, pounding his chest, "Henry Dunbar."

"Not Henry Dunbar, the Canadian media mogul!" asked Peter, seemingly all agog. "One of the world's richest, and arguably *the* world's most powerful man?"

"Yes, yes, that's me, or I, or at least my name— my grammar slips a little around certain ideas, spins around, around certain whirlpools. Anyway, according to that hateful traitor, my physician, it would be better to keep my tantrums 'to a minimum'; for my entourage not to engage with them, or appear to take them too seriously."

"Tantrums will be at a maximum tomorrow afternoon," Peter announced, "as Hurricane Henry moves through the Lake District. Viewers are advised to crawl into a basement and chain themselves to a rock."

Dunbar flailed his arms around, warding off more and more flies.

"I . . . I. Where was I? Oh, yes, after my little show of rage, Wilson remained impassive, thinking it was the right thing to do. Meanwhile, I noticed the egg; its surface turned out to be chipped and spoilt, but the interior was made of gold and the whole thing had failed to shatter in the way that my mood demanded. I walked over to it and brought my pitiless hell down on the maddening toy, but it was more resistant than I had imagined and the egg slid from under my shoe. I just caught the mantelpiece in time to save myself from an ignominious fall. I saw loyal Wilson rise from his chair and subside again. The moment of shock jolted me out of my fury and into a more fragile frame of mind.

"'I'm getting old, Charlie,' I said to Wilson, picking up the toy egg and pushing down the sense of dread I'd carried ever since that stupid, stupid accident in Davos: the constant fear of falling over again, of no longer being able to trust my treacherous body. 'I don't want that level of responsibility anymore,' I said. 'The girls will look after me, there's nothing they love more than fussing over their old father.'"

"In short," said Peter, in a thick Viennese accent, "'he turned his daughters into his mother!' As Freud said to the Bishop, on the corner of Heimatstrasse and Wanderlust."

"I opened the window nearest to me," Dunbar persisted, "and posted the egg into the air. 'That'll make someone's day,' I said.

"'As long as it doesn't crack their skull,' said Wilson. 'Heads are more brittle than gold.'"

"Oh, what a wise Wilson it is," said Peter.

"'I think we would have heard the cry of alarm by now,' I assured him, sitting back down behind my desk. 'People are better at hiding their glee than their agony. Here,' I said, offering Wilson a gift, 'why don't you have one of these? I've got enough of this Russki bling to make a Fabergé omelette.' I opened my drawer and tossed a glittering bauble through the air. Wilson, who had been playing catch with me and my family for several decades, since that first Sunday lunch when he found us all playing baseball in the garden like a normal family—like a family playing at being a normal family—caught it neatly, glanced down at the lattice of tiny diamonds that criss-crossed its crimson surface, and rolled it without comment onto the table beside his armchair, where it came to rest unsteadily next to his empty Meissen coffee cup."

"I'm loving the detail, darling," said Peter, the ecstatic theater director, "loving it."

"'You should at least hold back a block of shares,' said Wilson, 'and I'm telling you right now that you won't be allowed to keep Global One. No private citizen has his own 747.'

"'Allowed?' I thundered, *allowed*? Who is it will deny Dunbar his wishes? Who is it will deny Dunbar his whims?'"

"Why Dunbar, of course," said Peter. "Only he has the power, or had the power, or used to have the power."

"I'll make it a condition of the gift! By God, I'll have my way!"

A knock on the door made Dunbar fall abruptly silent. A hunted look came over his face.

"Quickly," said Peter, leaping up and hurrying to his side. "Remember, old man: pretend to take your meds, but don't swallow them," he whispered. "Tomorrow is the great escape, the great jailbreak."

"Yes, yes," whispered Dunbar, "the great escape. Enter!" he called out grandly.

Peter, who had started quietly humming the theme music of *Mission Impossible*, gave Dunbar a wink.

Dunbar tried to return the wink, but found he could not control his eyelids separately and blinked a few times instead.

Two nurses entered the room, pushing a trolley loaded with medicine bottles and plastic cups.

"Good afternoon, gentlemen," said Nurse Roberts, the older of the two. "How are we today?"

"Has it ever occurred to you, Nurse Roberts," asked Peter, "that we might have more than one emotion within us, let alone between us?"

"Up to your old tricks again, Mr. Walker," said Nurse Roberts. "Have we been to our meeting today?"

"We have been to our meeting, and I am happy to report that we experienced a warm sense of fellowship with our fellow fellows."

Nurse Muldoon couldn't help giggling.

"Don't encourage him," said Nurse Roberts with a disapproving sigh. "We're not going to try to run away to the pub again, are we?"

"What do you take me for?" asked Peter.

"A raging alcoholic," said Nurse Roberts sarcastically.

"What on earth could persuade a person to leave this notorious beauty spot," said Peter returning to his thespian tremolo, "this haven of natural tranquilizers, this valley through which the milk of human kindness flows like a silken river, healing the troubled minds of its already well heeled clientele?"

"Hmmm," said Nurse Roberts, "we've got our eye on you."

"Here at Schloss Meadowmeade," said Peter, metamorphosed into a German Kommandant, "we have ninety-nine point nine percent security! The only reason it is not one hundred percent is because you fellows locked one of your own officers on the window ledge overnight and he lost a finger to frostbite!"

"That's enough of your nonsense," said Nurse Roberts. "What's this vase doing on the floor? Nurse Muldoon, would you mind? And then, will you please accompany Mr. Walker back to his room. Mr. Dunbar needs his afternoon rest. It's time to say good-bye and let him get a little peace and quiet."

"See ya round, partner," said John Wayne, giving Dunbar a wink.

Dunbar blinked back several times to show that he understood.

After the others had left, Nurse Roberts led the way into the bedroom with her trolley.

"I don't think Mr. Walker is a good influence on you, personally," she said. "He just gets you agitated."

"Yes," said Dunbar humbly, "you're quite right, Nurse. He's a bit all over the place. I find him quite frightening sometimes."

"I'm not surprised you do, dear. To tell you the truth, I never liked *The Many Faces of Peter Walker*—always used to change channels. Give me Danny Kaye any day. It was a more innocent age. Or Dick Emery, oh, he used to make me laugh," said Nurse Roberts, plumping Dunbar's pillows while he sat on the edge of the bed, the very picture of a dazed old man.

"Now it's time for us to take our afternoon medicine," said Nurse Roberts. She set aside two bottles, lifting a plastic cup from the column of cups in the corner of the trolley.

"We've got our nice green and brown one that makes us feel all warm and fuzzy," she explained in language simple enough for poor old Dunbar to understand, "and then we've got our big white one that stops us having silly ideas about our daughters not loving us, when they're paying for us to have a lovely long holiday here at Meadowmeade, and to get the rest we deserve after being a very, very busy and very important man."

"I know they love me, really," said Dunbar, accepting the little cup. "I just get confused."

"Of course you do," said Nurse Roberts, "that's why you're here, dear, so we can help you."

"I have another daughter . . ." Dunbar began.

"Another daughter?" said Nurse Roberts. "Oh, dear, I'll have to have a word with Dr. Harris about your doses."

Dunbar tipped the pills into his mouth and took a sip of water from the glass proffered by Nurse Roberts. Smiling gratefully at his caregiver, he lay down on the bed and, without another word, closed his eyes.

"You have a nice little nap," said Nurse Roberts, wheeling her trolley out of the room. "Sweet dreams!"

The moment he heard the door close, Dunbar's eyes shot open. He sat up and spat the pills into his hand, hoisting himself out of bed and shuffling back into his sitting room.

"Monsters," he muttered, "vultures tearing at my heart and entrails." He pictured their ragged head feathers streaked with gore and offal. Treacherous, lecherous bitches, perverting his personal physician— the man appointed to examine Dunbar's body, authorized to take samples of Dunbar's blood and urine, to check him for prostate cancer, to shine torchlight onto his tender tonsils; it didn't bear thinking about, didn't bear thinking about—perverting his personal physician into their, into their *all too personal* gynecologist, their pimp, their copulator, their serpent dildo!

He thrust the pills down the neck of the vase with his shaking thumbs.

"You think you can castrate me with your chemicals, eh?" said Dunbar. "Well, you'd better watch out, my little bitches, I'm on my way back. I'm not finished yet. I'll have my revenge. I'll—I don't know what I'll do yet—but I'll . . ."

The words wouldn't come, the resolution wouldn't come, but the rage continued to swell up in him until he started to growl like a wolf preparing to attack, a low, slowly intensifying growl with nowhere to go. He hoisted the vase above his head, ready to fling it against his prison window, but then he froze, unable to smash it or to put it down, all action canceled by the perfect civil war of omnipotence and impotence that gridlocked his body and his mind.

2

"But why won't you tell me where he is?" said Florence. "He's my father, too."

"Darling, of course I'll tell you where he is," said Abigail, in a husky voice whose Canadian accent had been overlaid with the thick varnish of an English education. She wedged the phone in place with her tilted head while she lit a cigarette. "I just can't remember the name of the wretched place for the moment. I'll get someone to email it to you later today—promise."

"Wilson followed Henry to London because he was so worried about him," said Florence, "and got sacked the day he arrived. After forty years . . ."

"I know, isn't it dreadful?" said Abigail, gazing vacantly at sunlit blocks of Manhattan through the bedroom window. "Daddy's become so vindictive."

"Wilson said he had never seen him so upset," said Florence. "Apparently, he was raving at passers-by on Hampstead High Street after some kind of psychiatric evaluation you sent him to. The cash machines swallowed all his cards and when he discovered that his phone was cut off as well, he was so angry that he threw it under a passing bus. I don't understand how that could have happened."

"Well, you know how impatient he is."

"I don't mean that, I mean how his cards and his phone could—"

"Darling, he had a complete fit and was found by the police inside a hollow tree on Hampstead Heath, *talking to himself.*"

"If everyone who talked to themselves got put in a psychiatric hospital, there wouldn't be anyone left to look after them."

"Now, you're really beginning to annoy me," said Abigail. "Dr. Bob," she continued, smiling down at him, to savor the dramatic irony of his mention, "saw that Daddy was having a quite serious psychotic break."

Dr. Bob held up two thumbs to congratulate her on the use of this impressive phrase.

"And now he's been put in the very best and most comfortable sanatorium in Switzerland," said Abigail. "Oh, I wish I could remember its name, it's on the tip of my tongue. To be perfectly honest, when I saw the website," she confided, "I quite wanted to check myself in: it looked like *complete heaven*. I'm sorry if I sounded annoyed earlier, but it's not as if we love Daddy any less than you do; in fact, we've been at it rather longer than you, so we might arguably be said to love him more—from an accumulated income point of view. But seriously, markets still see him as the figurehead of the Trust and if a rumor gets out that Henry Dunbar has lost the plot, we could all wake up tomorrow with a couple of billion dollars wiped off the value of the shares, and another two the next day—that's all it takes: a rumor."

"I don't care about the share price; I just want to make sure that he's all right. If he's in trouble, I want to help."

"Oh, how noble of you!" said Abigail. "Well, some of us have already been helping him to run the Dunbar Trust, which, in case you hadn't noticed, is what he's actually been doing all our lives. I know you chose to opt out of that 'sordid power game' in order to become an artist and bring up your children in 'a sane environment.' God forbid you should pay attention to anything as crass as a share price—so long as your portfolio income comes rolling into your account every month."

"Oh, stop ranting, Abby. I just want to see him, that's all," said Florence. "Please email me the address as soon as you can."

"Of course I will, darling. Let's not argue, it's too . . . Oh, she's hung up," said Abigail, switching her phone off and sending it clattering onto the bedside table. "God, that girl gets on my nerves," she said, allowing her dressing gown to slip to the floor as she clambered back into bed. "I sometimes think I could kill her with my bare hands."

"I wouldn't do that," said Megan, who was lying on

the other side of Dr. Bob, looking dangerously bored. "Get a professional."

"Do you think we could get it off tax?" said Abigail. "'For professional services.'"

Megan, who was quite proud of her sullenness, nevertheless allowed herself a smile.

"Girls!" said Dr. Bob, in mock horror, "we're talking about your sister."

"Half-sister," Megan corrected him.

"We'd be perfectly happy if you'd surgically remove the part of her that's not a Dunbar, wouldn't we, Meg?"

"That seems like a very reasonable compromise," said Megan.

"She's got her mother's long legs," said Abigail.

"And her mother's eyes," said Megan.

"Anyhow, we only have to string her along for another five days, until the meeting on Thursday," said Abigail. "Then we'll have the Board behind us. It's time to strip Daddy of his role as 'non-executive chairman'— that was like asking for non-wet water—all those fucking memos!"

"I loved your email," said Megan, suddenly animated, "'Didn't you get the memo? DADDY IS GOING TO LIVE FOREVER.'"

"I know I shouldn't laugh," said Abigail, "but I can't help thinking of him on Hampstead High Street, shouting, 'Just make it happen! Just make it happen!'"

"That's the sum of his emotional intelligence to date," said Megan: "shouting, 'Just make it happen!'

and either having his way or getting someone sacked. Do you remember his face when we told him he couldn't have Global One to go to London?"

"'Why do you need a 747?' I asked," said Abigail. "'You can use one of the Gulfstreams—they're so much cosier.' I thought he was going to have a heart attack right there and then."

"'A Gulfstream,'" said Megan, impersonating her father, as if he were a petulant child. "'Who do you take me for? Who do you? Who do you *mistake* me for? One of the *merely* rich?'"

"He always told us not to be sentimental about business, and we're just doing what we were told," said Abigail obediently. "He certainly wasn't sentimental when it came to having Mummy sectioned during the custody battles. Well, now he can have a taste of his own medicine. And of your medicine," she added, as if Dr. Bob might be feeling left out. "What was it you gave him?"

"A non-specific disinhibitor. It was designed to make him more suggestible, basically more paranoid, if bad stuff was happening around him," said Dr. Bob, hoping the room was not bugged.

"It's rather pathetic that it took so little," said Megan. "Where are your inner resources, Dunbar?" she asked mockingly. "No money, no phone, no car, no entourage, a few harsh questions from our friend the psychiatrist, and a little bit of enhanced paranoia—that's all it took to drive him whimpering on to Hampstead Heath and cowering in a hollow tree."

"He was lucky to find a hollow tree," said Abigail,

like a nanny telling her little charge to stop complaining and start counting his blessings.

"The best bit is that he sacked his most loyal ally," said Megan. "It beggars belief. We would have had real trouble getting rid of Wilson, but to regretfully accept our father's last sane command and have his attorney removed from the Board is a dream come true."

"Well," said Dr. Bob, eager to move away from the subject of his former patient's downfall, "I just want to say that I must be the luckiest man in the world." He started to beat out a rhythm on his raised thighs, and then launched into a song from *Cabaret* that he hadn't been able to get off his mind.

" 'Beedle dee, dee dee dee,

Two ladies,

Beedle dee, dee dee dee,

Two ladies,

Beedle dee, dee dee dee,

And I'm the only man, ja!' "

"Please stop singing that awful song," said Megan. "The last thing we need is a theme tune for our expedient *ménage à trois*."

"That's right," said Abigail, pretending to stub and twist her cigarette in the imaginary ashtray of Dr. Bob's chest, but then resigning herself to using the real one on the bedside table.

"You two are as thick as thieves," said Dr. Bob. "A man could get to feel threatened around you."

"Don't deny that you enjoy feeling a little threatened," said Abigail, gripping one of his nipples and twisting it hard.

Dr. Bob caught his breath and closed his eyes.

"Harder!" he gasped.

Megan joined in hungrily, plunging her teeth into the other side of his chest.

"Jesus!" said Dr. Bob, "that's too much!"

Megan looked up at him, laughing.

"Jesus," he repeated, wriggling his way down the middle of the bed, away from the cruel parentheses of the women's reclining bodies.

"Sissy," said Abigail.

"Excuse me while I sew my nipple back on," said Dr. Bob. "I don't want to end up as the only man in America with an involuntary breast implant."

Picking up what appeared to be a luxurious brief-case rather than a medical bag, Dr. Bob hurried into the bathroom, naked. Looking in the mirror to assess the damage to his chest, he saw, through the strange blue tinge (such a delicate side effect) that stained his vision, the Viagra flush darkening his face. He was being wrecked by the demands of the voracious sisters. The side effect he dreaded most was priapism.

The inside of the case gave him an immediate and sorely needed sense of reassurance. In the upper half, small bottles of injectable liquids were held in place by leather belts with Velcro buckles: ketamine, diamorphine, and what he needed straight away, lidocaine hydrochloride, to anesthetize his chewed nipple while he sewed it back in place. He took out the bottle of lidocaine from the middle of the second row and placed it on the edge of the basin. A tray in the lower section of the case contained a set of instruments—scalpels, retractors, cannulas, a bone saw, a stethoscope, arterial clamps, and so forth—each nestling in its own purple velvet niche. He lifted the tray, revealing a lower layer of molded purple velvet, housing tightly packed rows of medication in uniform orange plastic cylinders. He shook out a couple of Percocet and knocked them back, and then on impulse, to counteract the narcotic effects of the painkiller, took a Dexedrine to keep him alert. A man couldn't afford to get dozy around the Dunbar sisters.

After injecting the lidocaine into his pectoral muscle, Dr. Bob opened a special compartment in his briefcase and took out a pair of powerful half-moon glasses. He switched on the band of light around the vanity mirror and started to examine the magnified and brightly lit wound. It was a tricky operation to perform on himself: keeping the wound open with forceps and then sewing its edges using a needle holder and black thread, but Dr. Bob's skill and experience soon resulted in a beautiful set of stitches with only a thin piece of thread emerging neatly from the end of the suture.

He marveled again at Megan's viciousness; she was the one who ought to be in a sanatorium, not her father. Dr. Bob could imagine (dimly) making a future with Abigail, except that she was getting too old and had the slightly absurd mannerisms of someone who had been over-impressed by the atmosphere of languid entitlement in her British boarding school. She was mostly amoral, sometimes conventionally moral, and often opportunistically immoral—in other words, normal, like him. Megan, on the other hand, was a fucking psychopath, whose displays of affection should be confined to a hospital that was equipped to deal with the consequences. In the end, he would dispense with them both. In the meantime, he had accepted their bribe of a seat on the Board, a six-and-a-half-million-dollar salary, and share options representing one point five percent of the Dunbar stock. That was his price for certifying that an eighty-year-old man in an artificially heightened state of anxiety was no longer fit to run one of the most complex business empires in the world. Not a bad deal. He had been slowly acquiring stock over the last twelve years. The old man used to give him some as a Christmas bonus, and he had invested all his spare money in the Trust as well.

A knock on the bathroom door made Dr. Bob reach for his roll of plaster, feeling the need for additional protection.

"Can I come in?" said Megan quietly, almost remorsefully.

"Okay," said Dr. Bob, hastily cutting a large section from the strip.

Megan walked into the bathroom and kissed him on the shoulder.

"I'm sorry, I know I went a bit too far," she said.

"I forgive you," said Dr. Bob.

She ran her nails lightly over his rib cage and down to his hip bone. The Viagra kicked into action.

"Here," said Megan, sitting on the edge of the marble counter and wrapping her legs around Dr. Bob's waist. "Take me here."

Dr. Bob put down the plaster and clasped the back of Megan's legs, just above the knee. She lowered her strong thighs on to his hands, trapping them on the counter and then, with one swift movement, like a bird of prey, she pecked at the wound in his chest with her sharp teeth.

"Got you," she said, laughing triumphantly.

Dr. Bob recoiled, dragging his hands free.

"You mad bitch!" he shouted.

"Don't ever talk to me like that," said Megan, "or I'll have you gutted like a fish."

Dr. Bob counted to ten, as he had so often fruitlessly advised Dunbar to do, in the hope of controlling his temper.

"I'm sorry," he said.

"I should hope so, too," said Megan, hopping down from the counter and standing in front of him. She pinched the tail of black thread protruding from his stitches and gave it a sharp tug.

"That's what you get for calling me horrid names," she said.

"I totally deserved that," said Dr. Bob, blood trickling from the reopened wound.

"Okay, my little lovebirds," said Abigail, putting her head round the bathroom door, "I've got to get back to my ghastly husband."

"And I have to get back to my husband's ashes," said Megan, slipping past her into the hall.

"Don't forget that you're coming to dinner tonight," said Abigail to Dr. Bob.

"How could I forget?" said Dr. Bob. How could he ever forget? The three of them were inseparable now, like mountaineers roped together at sunset on the same icy cliff face.

3

"Who am I?"

"You're Henry Dunbar, of course," said Nurse Roberts, opening the curtains.

"I don't mean my name, you stupid, stupid woman," growled Dunbar, "I mean who can tell me who I am, who I really am?"

"I don't appreciate being called stupid, thank you very much," said Nurse Roberts, "and who you 'really are' this morning is a very rude old man who owes Nurse Roberts an apology."

"I'm sorry, Nurse Roberts," said Dunbar, clinging to his fragmented sense that something very important was happening that day and that he must try to stay out of trouble.

"That's better," said Nurse Roberts. "We're only human and we all have mornings when we wake up on the wrong side of the bed, don't we?"

"We certainly do," said Dunbar, "almost every day."

"Now, are we going to have a lonely breakfast in

our room, or are we going to make the extra effort to go to the dining room and have a nice chat with some of the other guests?" asked Nurse Roberts.

"We're going to make the extra effort," said Dunbar.

"That's what I like to hear," said Nurse Roberts, throwing her weight behind Dunbar's unnecessary wheelchair and setting off through the thick carpet, as he leant back to smile at her pathetically.

Worried that his morning pills would start dissolving under his tongue, he faked a coughing fit and managed to spit them into his handkerchief. He was feeling more vigor without his meds, but also more rage and outrage. As the wheels of speculation and desire started to spin faster he could feel them generating more power, but he had no idea whether they could be stopped before they flew off altogether. He couldn't go back to the anguish he had felt after seeing that psychiatrist in Hampstead. Not that again, please, the feeling that there was nothing solid at all, that the ground he stood on was no more than a half-finished jigsaw puzzle, which was about to be pulled apart by a cruel and impatient child and that, worst of all, he was the child—there was no one else to blame for the treachery of everything; the horror, in the end, the horror was the way his mind worked.

"No outdoor activities for you today, not with that nasty cough," said Nurse Roberts. "I don't know why you've put on those great big boots. Wouldn't we be more comfortable in our slippers?"

"Not that again," muttered Dunbar. He couldn't

bear the encroaching madness, but he couldn't bear the encroaching asylum either. He needed Peter to help him get away. If he didn't escape today, he might never be able to leave; he might die with Nurse Roberts patting his hand, in a room full of stinking lilies.

"What was that, dear?"

He must keep his temper; he must be a perfect hypocrite. Dunbar, famous for his directness, famous for his strong opinions, famous for his startling mergers and acquisitions, must learn to be a hypocrite.

"No," said Dunbar. "I'll stay indoors today, huddled around the blue fire."

"The blue fire?" said Nurse Roberts, to whom the phrase sounded suspiciously pornographic.

"The television," said Dunbar. "It always looks like a blue fire flickering in the grate."

"Oh," said Nurse Roberts, relieved, "that makes it sound very comforting."

"It is comforting," said Dunbar, "especially if you own some of the channels and advertising revenues are going up because you have a hit show on your hands."

"Hmm," said Nurse Roberts, wheeling Dunbar into the dining room. "Remember what Dr. Harris said. There's no need to worry about business anymore, it's in safe hands now, and all we need to do is have a lovely long rest."

The dining room was part of the Victorian country house that formed the core of the sanatorium. Its William Morris wallpaper had been carefully copied and some of the oak tables were mainly original, but its dimensions, generous as they were for a large Victorian household, could not keep up with the modern demand for a place in which to neglect the mad, the old, and the dying. A vast conservatory extended beyond the gloomy old room, increasing the dining capacity but also offering a cheerful and light-filled social space, its armchairs and sofas upholstered in bold floral motifs, with leaves and flowers of Amazonian proportions trumpeting the healing powers of nature. Glass-topped bamboo tables, small round ones ready to receive a glass of mango juice and large rectangular ones already laden with as many creased magazines as any dentist's waiting room, were distributed among the tropical fabrics. In the summer the double doors opened on to a swaying meadow of tall grasses and wildflowers, but today the rain-beaded glass overlooked a field pitted with milky puddles, trampled stalks, and isolated tufts of dead grass. All year round, when it became visible in the intervals between fog and rain and snow, the rugged outline of a sublime lake completed the restful scene.

Dunbar scanned the room, looking for Peter Walker, but at the same time carefully avoiding the appearance of any eagerness to join a companion regarded by Nurse Roberts as a troublemaker and a thoroughly bad influence.

"Where would we like to go?" asked Nurse Roberts, answering her own question seamlessly, in case Dunbar had lost the power to speak. "We love the communal table, don't we? Because it's a chance to make new friends."

As she pushed him toward that precipice of haphazard social encounters, which Dunbar had so far managed to keep well away from, he glimpsed Peter standing by the conservatory's distant outer doors, under a green sign with the words Fire Exit written on it, next to a sprinting figure who must be trying to escape the inferno of Nurse Roberts's dating agency.

"Oh, you lucky man," said Nurse Roberts, almost indignant at so much good fortune being lavished on him, "there's a place for you next to Mrs. Harrod." She slid him into the empty space beside a conspicuously unhappy woman.

"I've completely lost my memory," said Mrs. Harrod, with the same acid self-assurance that she had shown in delivering the legendary put-downs that used to pepper her conversation. "Never apologize and never explain," she added with mechanical vehemence.

"Yeah, that's what accountants are for," said Dunbar, distractedly.

"Conversation," said Mrs. Harrod, "can be an Indian elephant, or an African elephant, but never both at the same time."

"Excuse me," mumbled Dunbar, seeing that Nurse Roberts was powering her way out of the room on another pharmaceutical or matchmaking mission, "I've just spotted a friend of mine." He rose to his feet, pushing back the obstructive wheelchair.

"I no longer enjoy coming to London; it's become like a foreign city," said Mrs. Harrod. And then she reached out and clasped Dunbar's arm.

"Am I going to die here, or am I going somewhere first?" she asked.

"I . . . I don't know," said Dunbar, recognizing the vertigo of the question.

"My father used to say that he was born into the diplomatic service," said Mrs. Harrod, regaining her poise for a moment, "making sure that his parents didn't argue all day long."

Dunbar removed her hand as gently as he could.

"Have I been to this place before?" she asked with piercing anguish.

Dunbar hurried away, without attempting to answer.

"Peter!" he started calling out, as he weaved his way toward the fire exit.

"Ah, there you are, old man," said Peter, turning around and pretending to punch Dunbar on the shoulder.

"Are we going to die here, or are we going somewhere first?" asked Dunbar.

"We're going somewhere first," Peter replied, setting off immediately. "To a pub in Windermere, or Grasmere, or Buttermere, or Meremere—I'm not going to argue about the details. My grasp of the local geography is a little shaky, but my passion for improving it is going to make Wordsworth look like a couch potato. Let's fetch our coats and scarves, and then throw our jailers off their guard by doubling back through the kitchens."

"The kitchens?" said Dunbar, trying to keep up with Peter as he hurried into the intricately tiled hall.

"Just act natural," said Peter, in a clenched-jawed parody of high anxiety that immediately made Dunbar feel nervous.

The two men found their overcoats on the numbered pegs where they belonged. Dunbar's immense black coat, almost too heavy to wield, with its double-breasted buttons and fur collar, contrasted with Peter's short green waterproof, with its Gore-Tex lining and sleek zip. While Dunbar wound several yards of cream cashmere around his neck, Peter tied a quick loop in a checkered Palestinian scarf.

"Yes, indeed, the kitchens," said thespian Peter. "Garry, the genius behind the Universal Sauce that glazes our every dish, without distinction of fish or fowl, not to mention the Cream of Soup, which makes it quite impossible, in a blind test, to tell the difference between the pea, the carrot, and the leek—my esteemed friend Garry allows me to pass through the kitchen to smoke an illicit cigarette. *Just act natural*," he whispered urgently.

"Please stop saying that, it's making me anxious," said Dunbar.

"What's making *me* anxious," said Peter, "is cash. Mine was confiscated as part of my 'treatment.' Ill treatment," intoned thespian Peter, "masquerading as treatment for the ill."

"I don't have any cash," said Dunbar, "and my cards have been canceled."

"What?" cried Peter, horrified. "But you're a multibillionaire. I wasn't expecting you to have a rabbit trap, to help us live off the land, or a hang glider, to take us from this fell hell, with its pretentious puddle of a lake, into the cobbled streets of a proper lakeside village packed with picturesque pubs, but I was counting on you for cash."

"There is one card," said Dunbar, with furtive excitement, "that those thieving bitches didn't know about—a Swiss account."

"The Swiss account," said Peter, jumping up and down. "What's the limit?"

"There is no limit," said Dunbar, suddenly frightened.

"No limit!"

"Please stop saying that," said Dunbar.

"We can hire a limo," said Peter, putting his arm around Dunbar and leading him toward the swinging kitchen doors, "and get the hell out of this National Park. We can go to London! We can go to Rome and drink Negronis among some of the world's greatest ruins!"

"I don't want the ruins," said Dunbar, with a pulse of his old authority, "I want the empire back."

"Of course you do, old man," said Peter, leading Dunbar into the kitchen, with his arm still round his shoulder, "and back you shall have it."

"Hello, Peter," said Garry.

"Maestro!" said Peter. "Behold the Escoffier of the Lakes!" he said to Dunbar.

"Off to have one of your fags, are you?" said Garry, scraping amorphous bricks of scrambled egg into a silver dish.

"I try to kick the habit, but the habit kicks harder," said Peter.

"All right then," said Garry, "but you've got to do your Orson Welles first."

"My Orson Welles?" said Peter, in a perfect impersonation. "Why, I don't know what you mean." He staggered back two steps, looking from side to side, as if the great actor might be nearby, and then came to rest heavily against the stainless steel counter.

"Do not ask me what I want to eat," he said, with the rich modulations of Welles's Othello, wavering eloquently between love and revenge, "when you know what I *must* eat." He paused and then cried out, in a voice freighted with grief, "Grilled fish!"

"Grilled fish," said Garry, chuckling. "That always gets me."

"He wouldn't have been allowed one of your delicious sauces," said Peter, "because he was on a diet. That was a quotation from something he said to a waiter in Los Angeles, when he was having lunch with Gore Vidal."

"So, it's a bit of history, then," said Garry.

"I'll let you in on a little secret, Garry: everything is history. By the time you notice it, it's already happened. That famous imposter, 'the present,' disappears in the cognitive gap. Mind the gap!" cried Peter, like a stationmaster warning passengers as train doors open.

"Please don't say that," pleaded Dunbar, leaning on the counter for support.

"All right then," said Garry, "you go and have your smoke, but when you get back you've got to do your Leonardo di Caprio for me."

"That's quite a tax rate you've got me on," said Peter, trying to guide the bewildered Dunbar toward the back door.

"Well, it's the price of success, isn't it, Peter?" said Garry.

"You've got a deal," Peter called out, as he turned the handle.

"Don't let that man cheat you," said Dunbar, "there's no need to pay more than an average of seven percent tax, if you get yourself organized."

"Maybe," said Peter, zipping up his coat as the cold air defeated warmth on the threshold of the kitchen, "but I want more than seven percent of the hospital to be there when I get myself disorganized—in a car crash, for instance."

"Do we have a reliable driver?" asked Dunbar, alarmed by the vivid scene of mutilation that the words "car crash" formed in his imagination. He pictured his broken and bleeding body among the buckled metal and scattered glass, and the ambulance men standing by, looking at his tax return and shaking their heads. He hadn't contributed enough to the Exchequer, he hadn't honored his side of the social contract, he hadn't given enough; they were going to leave him there to bleed to death.

Peter put his finger to his lips and frowned.

Dunbar suddenly remembered what they were

doing. He had drifted off somewhere. Why had he mentioned the driver? He might have ruined everything. He felt like a fool, an utter fool. His mother used to frown at him like that; it was all she had to do to get her way. He thought he had forgotten the rule of shame, until his recent troubles blasted open those old mineshafts, long filled with the rubble of power and money. Now Peter's frown was burning into him and making him want to become invisible, as if all those decades he had spent becoming more and more conspicuous, becoming Henry Dunbar, becoming a household name, were just impediments to a much deeper longing to disappear. What was going on? How could he forget himself like that? His sense of self was so fragile and contingent; it might dissolve like a watercolor in the rain.

"I'm sorry, I'm sorry," he said, following Peter outside, afraid he wouldn't be allowed to come along because he was such an old fool. "I'm sorry. Am I allowed to come? Am I allowed?"

"Of course you are, old man," said Peter. "I just didn't want anyone to catch on to our plans. They don't like inmates to under-stay their welcome in this gulag. Jesus, it's cold, I wish we did have a car and a reliable driver, but we're going to have to walk. Cumbria in December—people flock here just for the hailstorms. It's standing room only on Scafell Pike."

The two men walked past giant color-coded recycling bins toward a woodland path that offered the most discreet escape, cutting into the lane well below

the driveway of the sanatorium. As they left the court-
yard, they saw a quad utility vehicle parked behind
the wall, with the keys still in the ignition.

"How powerful are thy Thoughts, Oh, Mighty
One!" said Peter, in epic voiceover. "In the beginning
was the Thought, and the Thought was with Dunbar,
and Dunbar thought *car* and behold there was a car,
and he saw that it was good."

"Did I really do that?" said Dunbar incredulously,
getting onto the bench next to Peter. "But what would
happen if I thought something bad?"

"Don't worry, Henry, it's not a perfect system: you
haven't manifested a reliable driver, for instance.
Nobody has ever accused me of being one of those,
especially when I go over the alcohol limit, which I
sincerely hope to do later today, by a factor of at least
twenty."

The noisy engine puttered into action and the quad
lurched forward, toward the wood. As they bounced
along the narrow, muddy path, Peter morphed into a
car bore, shouting technical information with boyish
enthusiasm over the roar of the engine, but Dunbar
was not listening. He was considering the question of
his special powers. He had always suspected he had
some, but now that he had manifested the very vehicle
that they needed in order to escape across this wild
land, he was completely convinced for the first time.
He felt the rush of destiny, like electricity shimmering
down through his body from head to foot. He closed
his eyes and experienced a moment of perfect seren-

ity. He would get everything back and, with his power restored, he would punish his wicked daughters and leave the empire to Florence. He had always known that he was supposed to love his children equally, but couldn't disguise that it was Florence who charmed and delighted him. She had inherited her mother's beauty as well as her disarming sympathy. Just by listening to him, she could make the knots he tied himself in spontaneously loosen and unravel. She didn't exercise this effect self-consciously; it was a natural phenomenon, like ice melting at a certain temperature. Apart from her virtues, he loved Florence simply because she was Catherine's daughter, and Catherine was the great love of his life, a love, or at least an image of love, immortalized by death, sealed off from decay and habituation, from the mundane forces that turn admiration into tolerance, and tolerance into irritation. He could see now, in this moment of lucidity, that after Catherine was killed in the car accident, he had clung to Florence in a way that may have contributed to her desire for independence and her decision to have nothing more to do with his business. At the time he could only see it as a rejection and a second loss, a view encouraged by his other daughters, who had always resented his favoritism, and had spared no effort to please him by imitating his ruthlessness and his will to power. They persuaded him that Florence's shares must be taken away and given to them, the loyal daughters who respected his achievement and would carry on his legacy. How blind he had been.

In a way, he could see now that Florence was the one with the real stubbornness and pride. She had just walked away and never faltered.

Surprised to feel the quad slow down, Dunbar opened his eyes and saw Mrs. Harrod standing in the middle of the path, beside a mossy outcrop of gray rock, waving them down. Peter was forced to stop.

"Are you a taxi?" asked Mrs. Harrod, coming round to Peter's side.

"Ursula!" said Peter. "Which way are you headed?"

"I want to go home."

"That's where we're going, too!" said Peter. "Have you got the fare?"

"I have my emergency money," said Mrs. Harrod, pulling a crumpled envelope out of her overcoat pocket. Peter counted three fifty-pound notes.

"The exact fare!" he said, tucking the envelope into his jacket. "Hop aboard."

"We can't take her," whispered Dunbar, "she's as mad as a snake."

"Henry, Henry," said Peter reproachfully, "we're in a part of the world famous for its 'little, nameless, un-remembered acts of kindness and of love.' In any case, once you set sail in a ship of fools, there's never any shortage of passengers!"

"But there is a shortage of room," said Dunbar, moving reluctantly along the bench.

"Aha!" said Peter. "It's a sign!"

He pointed to a sign with the words Plumdale (Bridle Path Only) written on it.

"With the traction on this baby," said Peter, "we

can handle the bridle path, but our jailers won't be able to follow us in their cumbersome convoy of ordinary cars."

As the quad set off again, roaring along the new woodland path, Dunbar's mood collapsed without warning or transition. He realized that he couldn't rely on Peter, who was just off on a drunken escapade, and he certainly couldn't rely on the demented Mrs. Harrod. He was going to have to escape alone. The leafless trees, with their black branches stretching out hysterically in every direction, looked to him like illustrations of a central nervous system racked by disease: studies of human suffering anatomized against the winter sky.

4

Florence stared at the glittering jets surging from the fountain in the Central Park reservoir, but instead of being thrilled by their abounding energy she found herself mesmerized by the power of gravity dragging the water down after its brief ebullience, like a scolding father killing a child's high spirits with a curt remark. She slid open the doors of the terrace and walked back into her drawing room. She had gone outside to escape the heat, and now she was going back inside to escape the cold. Soon she would be too hot again. Nothing was right; nothing could cure her restlessness. Uneasy after her conversation with Abigail, she had come straight to New York to confront her sisters about where they had hidden her father, but they had slipped away as she arrived and continued to ignore her messages and emails. Only Mark, Abigail's guilty and alienated husband, was left in the city. She had called him last night, but he had no idea where Dunbar was, or even where Abigail had gone.

"All they've told me," said Florence, "is that Henry is in a clinic somewhere in Switzerland."

"Well, at least that's one country you can rule out," said Mark, with what he intended to be a hollow laugh but only qualified as a grunt. "Even when there's no need to, Abby lies ferociously. As you know, she thinks that telling the truth is a weakness. The truth is, roughly speaking, usually one thing—either Henry is in Switzerland or he isn't—but lying is potentially infinite and so it wards off the thing those girls dread most: monotony."

"I guess you're right."

"Come on, Flo," said Mark, "this is the sister who weakened the props on your rocking horse, hoping they would snap while you were riding high, and that your neck would follow suit."

"It was hard for her, my mother was there, and hers was—"

"You're too forgiving," Mark interrupted, "I live with her. The first time she told me that story, I thought I was supposed to admire her honesty, or the way she transcended her difficult childhood; now I realize that she was boasting about early signs of greatness."

"Well, why do you stay with her?" asked Florence.

"Fear," said Mark. "She has to be the one who wants to end it; if I do, she'll find a way to destroy me."

Florence could think of nothing to say. The conversation concluded with a hedged promise from Mark that he would help, if he could do so "without ending up in a sanatorium of my own."

Mark's use of "sanatorium" as a Soviet euphemism for savage incarceration made Florence regret having spoken to her emasculated brother-in-law. Her father's disappearance was making her unbearably aware that if he died before they were reconciled, she would be left with the memory of a relationship overwhelmed by disappointment and disapproval, like that crashing, downcast fountain in the park. He had doted on her until a year ago, letting her believe that she would always win the competition for his favor, against her sisters, against the Board members, against his friends and suitors, and against his forty thousand employees, but when she admitted that she didn't want anything to do with the family business, and wanted to go off with Benjamin and the children to lead what was supposed to be a simple life in wild Wyoming, Dunbar was overtaken by one of his rages, removing her from the Board, cutting her out of his will, and spitefully excluding her children from the Trust. He treated her indifference to business as a personal insult, as well as an immaturity that, given time, would have dissolved in the atmosphere of self-importance that suffused his organization, the feeling that history was not just being witnessed but created by his media empire. She knew that history must be something more than a gleefully tendentious version of the news, but it was not on that argument that her relationship with Henry foundered. She understood that her father was being so harsh because her independence was not only a rejection of his legacy but also of her role as a surviving fragment of her mother.

She was only capable of being independent because she had been adored in the first place, but a man as possessive as her father could not experience her autonomy as a compliment, or protect himself from mistaking her sisters' acquisitiveness for love.

Florence had been sixteen when her mother died. For a long time afterward she felt her own existence contracting loyally around her mother's absence. At the same time the meaning of her mother's death expanded uncontrollably, until it seemed to explain the moods of her teachers, the taste of her food, and the color of the grass. Slowly, after a year of paralysis, forgotten memories of her mother started to circulate in Florence's dreams and in conversations with people who remembered Catherine's remarks and stories and gestures. She became alive again in her daughter's mind. For Henry this had never happened. His wife was frozen and idealized, while Florence was given the job of perpetuating the qualities he admired in her. It was what Henry Dunbar was used to: mergers and acquisitions, delegation and rebranding. Florence was merged with Catherine's ghost, rebranded as the companion, best friend, sweet-natured woman, and heir apparent that his psyche required. When she chose her husband over her father, and the next generation over the last, she knew that in his eyes she was heartlessly destroying his last defense against acknowledging Catherine's complete extinction. Given his temperament, she was not surprised that he preferred to turn his grief into rage. What she didn't anticipate was how long he would resist any reconciliation, and that one of them might die before it was achieved.

Even while he was ranting, calling her names that would have been unforgivable if she hadn't regarded his fits as a kind of incidentally verbal epilepsy, her father must have known that he couldn't reduce Florence to the penury she deserved. Although she was a pauper by Dunbar standards, she had more than enough money not to submit to him on financial grounds. She already owned the apartment she was in right now; she had inherited her mother's fortune (which, as he reminded her, cursing his misguided generosity, she really owed to him, as she owed *everything* to him) and she was also the beneficiary of a satellite trust that he had created for his children and which Wilson told him was impossible to break, or to exclude her from. She had given him back her Dunbar shares without protest, or payment, humiliating him with her generosity.

Florence slid open the doors and stepped back onto the terrace, half marveling at how predictable she was, and half wondering if she was doing what she predicted in order to prove herself right. She had been up most of the night, watching the clock creep forward toward a time when she could allow herself to phone Wilson. He had managed to protect her over the last year, while continuing to be her father's most loyal ally, but after being sacked, Wilson had retreated with his wife and family to his holiday place near To-fino, on Vancouver Island, where it was still far too early to call him. Just as she was yet again calculating how long she would have to wait, her phone rang and Wilson's name appeared on the screen.

"Wilson! I was just thinking it was still too early to call you."

"I've been holding back for a couple of hours myself. When I heard last night that nobody can get hold of Henry I was too worried to sleep."

"Do you have any idea where he is?"

"I've got a team of interns ringing private hospitals and clinics all over Europe and North America, asking for him by name, and also with the aliases he uses to check into hotels incognito. So far, nothing."

"How can I help?" asked Florence.

"We've only got four days until the decisive Board meeting. I've been phoning around, but it seems like your sisters have fixed their majority. Most of the Board are sound people chosen by your father with my help, but they've been shown the key document I urged him not to sign, giving all the real power to Abby and Megan, and now they've got Dr. Bob's report, which is going to be used to justify his dismissal as non-executive chairman. Your sisters want to get him out of the picture completely. He still has too much influence, his presence is enough to make the Board look for ways to please him, even though he doesn't have any legal power of his own."

"If he's unfit to run his affairs, there should be a power of attorney. I'm sure he would have given that to you."

"He did, but it was conditional on my employment, and your father really did sack me. You can guess who my replacements are."

"But couldn't we argue—" Florence began.

"It doesn't work," Wilson interrupted. "Even if we got me the power of attorney back, your sisters could sack me a minute later, once their position has been confirmed by the Board."

"God, it sounds like they've got this coup sewn up."

"It's bewildering—nobody understood power better than your father. For the last forty years he's operated on every continent, and for at least half of that time he's been able to highlight, spin, or bury a story, get hold of any world leader he wants to talk to, influence elections, and destroy his enemies. And then one day he woke up and just wanted the toys instead of the real thing. I was astonished, he'd never been impressed by any of that before, but whatever happened to make him lose his focus, none of it justifies the abduction and humiliation, and . . ."

"And what?"

"I don't know; I don't know what they're capable of, but I know that I've never seen your father as frightened as he was that day in Hampstead. He was having a panic attack. He was frightened of the sky, he was frightened of the light; he seemed to have agoraphobia—this is the man who bought a million-acre ranch in New Mexico because he loves big skies."

"I feel like someone who's been woken by a fire alarm," said Florence, "as if my life with Benjamin has been an expensive fantasy taking place while my sisters hijacked the Trust and kidnapped my father."

"It may be time to put on your Dunbar armor."

"Oh, believe me, it's on and it's not coming off until he's safe."

"I can only see one weakness, and one long shot. The weakness is Mark. He has a conscience of sorts, but most of all he's grown to despise Abby. He might be prepared to say things to a beloved sister-in-law that he wouldn't say to an ex-attorney."

"Forget it, I've already called him, and he's too scared."

"Still, it may be worth spending a couple of hours with him and listening to what he tells you. Perhaps he can't act against Abby directly, but I know he's very torn and he might give you some hints."

"What's the long shot?" asked Florence.

"Do you remember Jim Sage, the pilot of Global One?"

"Of course, he tried to teach me to fly."

"If they took the plane, he'll know where they landed. He would naturally just tell you, unless he's been forbidden to. They might not have anticipated that approach. I'm emailing you his cell number right now."

"Okay, I'll call him after we've finished."

"I'll be in New York by this evening. I'm coming with Chris; Henry was always a good godfather to him and he wants to help. There's a seaplane collecting us in twenty minutes and taking us to Vancouver. I'd better get my things and head down to the jetty."

"Thanks for doing this, Charlie. You could have just retired after the way you were treated."

"That's what my wife wants, but I'm not ready for a life of storm watching, interspersed with visits to UNESCO world heritage sights. I'm going to fight to get your father back in charge and fight for a decent transition that protects the forty thousand people who work for the Trust. And, to be completely honest, I don't want to see your sisters win."

After the call, Florence felt that pacing the terrace was not enough; she had to go into the Park to work out her anxiety and decide how far she needed to get involved in the family politics she had walked away from so zealously only a year ago. There seemed to be no way to secure her father's safety without getting entangled in a war with her sisters, putting pressure on a divided brother-in-law, marshaling arguments to sway the Board. And yet what she had said to Wilson was true: she had already put on her armor, she was already at war, and the decision felt all the deeper for having worked its way through her apparently gentle nature like an underground, winter-born river that only emerges from a hillside after heavy rain, but then sweeps boulders away and uproots trees.

The cinder paths in the Park, whose curvature was as remorseless as the grid of streets that surrounded them, annoyed Florence in a way that would have struck her friends and family as uncharacteristic. They seemed to insist that she was now at leisure, that recreation must meander and postpone, in contrast to the dumb practicality of tracing the shortest distance between two points, but she had no desire to make charming detours, to be told to relax and enjoy the journey; she wanted to get to the point, she wanted to take action to save her father. She cut across the grass, defining her own path, and as she walked, she found Wilson's email on her phone and tapped on Jim Sage's number.

"Hello."

"Jim? This is Florence, Florence Dunbar."

"Hey, Florence, it's good to hear your voice," said Jim affectionately. "What can I do for you? Have you decided to learn to fly, after all?"

"How did you guess?" said Florence, improvising. "I had such a lousy trip here yesterday; it reminded me of what you said about getting my own license. Are you free at all? I'm in New York right now. Perhaps we could schedule something."

"I'd love to do that, Florence, only I'm in Manchester and I don't know when we're headed back. Your sisters are kind of spontaneous with the itinerary compared to Mr. Dunbar."

"Manchester?" said Florence. "What are you doing there?"

"I have no idea. It's not for me to reason why, but all I can tell you is the weather here is dark and dismal."

"Well, when you're back, let's get airborne," said Florence, drawing the conversation to a close as quickly as possible, in the hope of getting hold of Wilson before he was engulfed by the roar and the shudder of one of those old seaplanes.

"It's a deal," said Jim.

She hung up and immediately made her next call.

"Florence!" said Wilson, over the sound of lapping water. "I'm just getting on the plane."

"Manchester," said Florence. "I spoke to Jim and he told me that's where they landed. Tell the interns to concentrate on England, especially places closer to Manchester than London."

"Will do," said Wilson. "Good work. They're about to start the engines, but Chris wants me to send his love."

"Send him mine," said Florence, allowing herself to smile for the first time in several days.

5

The King's Head was set back from the shores of Merewater by a patch of lawn with a flagpole planted at its center. To Dunbar, sitting in the bay window of the bar, the rope on the flagpole looked as if it could barely keep hold of its writhing flag, a St. George's Cross tormented by a whistling onshore wind, which also lashed the black waters of the lake into nervous white waves and dashed them hurriedly onto the rocks of a narrow beach at the foot of the hotel. To mark the outer edge of the lawn swags of heavy black chain hung between thick white posts, echoing the color scheme of the water as well as the untouched Guinness in front of him on the table. Outside in and inside out, from lake to glass and glass to lake, and in between a chain, on which he could all too easily imagine himself tripping and being pitched forward onto the rocks; his precious, unreliable brains spilling out; the waves lapping hungrily; his blood the color of the cross on the flag, trembling and wrinkling in the wind.

Dunbar clasped the table for support. There were too many dismembering resemblances between one thing and another. He must try to keep things in their proper place, the lake in the lake, the beer in the glass, the blood in his body.

"Another round!" said Peter boisterously, rising to his feet.

Although Mrs. Harrod had only taken a sip of her ginger wine, and Dunbar had not yet embarked on his glass of Guinness, Peter's own pint of Guinness was dry, and he had already drunk the three large whiskies he ordered for himself on arrival, pretending they each wanted one.

He hastened to the bar, radiating charm.

"We would all like another large Famous Grouse, and two more pints of Guinness, please. The lady is still 'working on' her ginger wine."

He threw in a request for an assortment of sandwiches and placed a fifty-pound note on the counter, patting it repeatedly both to draw attention to his willingness to pay for his bold order, and also from a half-conscious reluctance to part with the money. It was the second of Mrs. Harrod's fifties, and there was only one left. There would of course be some change from the first hundred, but he really needed to start encouraging Dunbar to check out his Swiss credit card. If that wasn't working, he should ditch the others and try to find an off-license instead of wasting his money in bars. He needed to get properly drunk, he was at that point in the cycle, he needed to navigate through blackout, to give impulsive performances to amazed strangers and to end up somewhere inexplicable, deranged in a city he didn't know, in a room he didn't recognize; if not free, at least severely disoriented.

"I'll bring everything over, sir," said the barman.

"I'll carry the whiskies," said Peter helpfully.

Back at the table, he poured the three doubles into one glass.

"I've always despised the imperial measures," said Peter. "If we can make it to The World of Beatrix Potter, which I know is temptingly nearby, we can probably see the adorable little thimble that constitutes the original 'single' measure, carefully chosen to be exactly the right amount of whisky for a newborn squirrel, or a parsimonious dormouse."

"Oh, I love Beatrix Potter," said Mrs. Harrod. "Do let's."

"*This* is what I call 'a shot,'" said Peter in his John Wayne voice, holding up his voluminous whisky before knocking it back in one gulp. He put down the empty glass, unimpressed, but not displeased.

"Doesn't that hill look just like a Christmas pudding?" said Mrs. Harrod, pointing to a rounded hill on the far side of the lake, "with a sprinkling of icing sugar on top."

"Hang on," said Dunbar, disturbed by the further turmoil of resemblance suggested by Mrs. Harrod's comparison.

"You're right," Peter interrupted, "with that rusty winter bracken and the dusting of snow. You've certainly got an eye for giant puddings, Ursula. Has anybody ever told you that?"

"No, they haven't," said Mrs. Harrod bashfully.

"Well, it's true," said Peter.

"Now, listen!" insisted Dunbar, trying to master his anxiety with a show of indignation, "we're not going to some fucking Beatrix Potter museum, or climbing up a Christmas pudding; we're going to get a car to London and we're going to get this whole situation *under control.*"

"Absolutely, old man," said Peter reassuringly. "Let me take this off your hands before it gets warm and flat," he said, picking up Dunbar's glass and draining half the contents. "There's a fresh one on its way and it's high time this one got dispatched." He finished the pint with a theatrical smacking of the lips. "What we have to find out is whether that Swiss card of yours is working so we can make a taxi driver an offer he can't refuse."

"Don't talk about my card in public," hissed Dunbar, leaning across the table, "it's a secret account."

"Your secret is safe with Ursula," said Peter.

"What secret?" said Mrs. Harrod. "What were we talking about?"

Peter smiled complacently at Dunbar, but the old man was not appeased.

"By the way, Ursula," said Peter, "does your emergency money need refreshing? Since Henry and I are going to a cashpoint, perhaps I could get some more for you."

"They don't let me have a card anymore because I can't remember the number."

"Fiends," said Peter. "Unfeeling monsters."

"Did your daughters take your cards away as well?" asked Dunbar.

"No, it was my bank," said Mrs. Harrod. "I think it's quite sensible; goodness knows what I'd do if I had one."

When the sandwiches and beer arrived, Peter was tempted to order more whisky, but instead managed to ask the barman where the nearest cashpoint was.

The two men wolfed down their food.

"I never go to London these days," said Mrs. Harrod. "It's become like a foreign city."

"Well, in that case, you'll be pleased to hear that we won't be dragging you there today," said Dunbar drily.

Peter sat down next to Mrs. Harrod and took her hand.

"Now, Ursula, you hold the fort while we go to get some cash. We'll be back soon."

"Where are we?" said Mrs. Harrod.

"The King's Head," said Dunbar, "we're in the King's Head."

"Do you want this?" asked Peter, pointing to Dunbar's glass.

"No, you have it," said Dunbar impatiently, "you seem to like it well enough."

"Ah, I've a terrible thirst on me," said Peter in a thick Irish accent. "There's a fire raging in my troubled mind and there's only one thing in this sorry world can extinguish it."

"Oh, you poor man," said Mrs. Harrod, "you must get some professional help."

"Well, thanks to Dr. Guinness here," said Peter, winking broadly at Mrs. Harrod, "I'm already feeling much better, thank you kindly."

There was only one bank in Plumdale High Street, a few hundred yards down the hill from the King's Head, just after a bend in the road. It had a cashpoint inside as well as one on the pavement.

"Let's go indoors, it'll be warmer," said Peter.

"They might have CCTV," said Dunbar.

"With your daughters watching on the Northern Rock Bank Channel," said Peter, knowingly.

"That's exactly what I'm afraid of," said Dunbar.

"I see," said Peter. "Well, let's stay in the unsupervised streets, ignoring this meat cleaver of a wind and those black clouds squabbling over who gets to rain first."

Wrapped in his fur-collared overcoat, Dunbar was impervious to these meteorological threats and, as he extracted the Swiss credit card from his wallet, he seemed to enter into a kind of trance. He slipped the card into the slot with a solemnity that Peter had never seen in him before. He grew in stature as he chose various options on the screen and tapped in his personal identification number, shielding it from Peter's inquisitive gaze, and yet it was only after his request for five hundred pounds was answered by the sound of the notes being counted by the automatic teller that he drew himself to his full height, back in command of the money that both men craved, and with which he was so inextricably identified in the eyes of the world, as well as in his own estimation. It reminded Peter of watching a flame being injected from the burner of a hot air balloon into the sagging, wrinkled fabric of the envelope, until it swelled and stretched upward, tugging at the tethered gondola.

"Success!" said Dunbar, pulling the cash from the flashing teeth of the machine.

"Excellent," said Peter, clapping his hands, and jumping up and down, as if he'd turned into the balloon that he'd just been imagining. "Try it again! We're three hundred miles from London, who knows what a car service would charge for a limo on a journey like that?"

"Between two and three pounds a mile," said Dunbar.

"Well, there you go, we need twice as much cash, you've only got enough to get us to Birmingham."

"I'll pay with the card," said Dunbar, "it's got . . ." he hesitated.

"No limit!" said Peter. "No limit!"

Dunbar closed his eyes to shut out the images that were washing over him, but they only grew stronger: a snapping cord, an astronaut disconnected from the mother ship and sent flipping through the frigid darkness, surrounded by stars so far away they might have ceased to exist by the time their dim lights were reflected in his visor. As the ship disappears, all directions are abolished, there is no gravity, no tangible surface or meaningful reference point, only the hollow scepter of infinite space: forty-one thousand two hundred and fifty-three square degrees of indifference.

He felt Peter's arm encircling his shoulder and gently turning him back toward the cashpoint. Too shocked by his hellish vision to protest, he stumbled through the motions of another withdrawal and made no effort to stop Peter from extracting the second wad of twenty-pound notes and stuffing them into his own trouser pocket.

"Don't worry, old man, I've got the money," said Peter, guiding Dunbar back up the street. "We're all set up for the journey. We'll just head back to the hotel and order up the best limo service Plumdale has to offer. It may be a car with a bar, plenty of legroom, and a lap pool, or it may be a mobile sheep dip, but one way or another we're off to London Town, the Big Smoke, the Capital of the World!"

As they rounded the bend in the street, Peter thrust out his arm abruptly, knocking the bewildered Dunbar in the chest.

"Double back, double back," said Peter. "I saw a Meadowmeade van outside the King's Head. They're probably waterboarding poor Ursula right now to find out what she knows. With her memory issues we might have been safe—if only we hadn't asked the barman for the nearest cashpoint! Hurry up, for God's sake."

Peter pounded down the pavement, past the incriminating bank and took the first side street he could. Dunbar followed, but as they rounded the corner of Merewater Lane he pleaded for a slower pace.

"Okay," said Peter, "take your time; just keep heading downhill toward the lake. This is a dead end for cars, but I'll go ahead and see if there's a way out on foot. Otherwise, it's going to be a day at the funfair for Nurse Roberts, shooting us with tranquilizing darts through the open window of the van."

"Please don't say that," said Dunbar, "it's too vivid."

"Don't worry, old man, we'll find a way," said Peter. "We may have to wade back to the King's Head along the shore, and then take a couple of rooms for the night. It's the last place they'll think of searching for us, once they've left there empty-handed!"

Before Dunbar could raise the obvious objections to this scheme, Peter dashed down the lane on his exploratory mission. Neither man had a phone. Dunbar's had been crushed under the wheels of a London bus, and Peter, after his persistent escape attempts, had been forced to surrender his as a condition of remaining at Meadowmeade, itself a condition of securing a new series of *The Many Faces of Peter Walker*. If only Dunbar had a phone, he would order a taxi right away. He had taken everything in: they were in Merewater Lane, in Plumdale. He might not be fast, but he was practical and he was as strong as a bull. He had always spent the Canadian part of his winters cross-country skiing and the Canadian part of his summers taking long swims in his own lake, a rather larger body of water than the one opening up in front of him as he came to the end of the lane.

"Henry! This way!" said Peter, reappearing through a small gate to Dunbar's right. "Quickly, let's get out of sight before our jailers come down the lane."

Dunbar hurried through the gate and followed his elated companion along the path.

"It's perfect," said Peter. "I've seen a big plastic map ruggedly mounted on some local timber: we're on a public footpath that runs around the lake. They'll never find us here; it's wooded and full of forking paths. If we headed for the hills now, we'd be too conspicuous, but at the other end of the lake we can climb up to a pass that takes us into the next valley."

Dunbar assented with a grunt. He was locking into his walking stride, preserving his energy, refusing to disperse himself in speculative chatter, absorbed by a single objective: to get to London and somehow take back control of the Trust. His body had a sanity that had recently been eluding the rest of him. He could feel its stubbornness and the way his attention was starting to fall in with its narrow sense of purpose. That was just what he needed in order to combat the feeling of—he mustn't think about it—there being no limits. He mustn't think about that, but you had to think about something to know what it was you were not thinking about. All his life he had focused, some might say, psychological types might say, fixated on one thing—a deal, a merger, sometimes a woman—without wondering why; it had just seemed inevitable, irresistible, self-explanatory, but now he knew why, he really knew why. He had been like a dog plunging into the water to retrieve a stick, or like a hawk falling out of the sky to claw a sparrow, because the alternative was that hurtling emptiness with no direction and no home. Oh, God, he didn't want to think about it. Hadn't he already said that he didn't want to think about it? Why was nobody paying attention to his instructions? All four secretaries away from their posts, paring their fingernails, while he barked down the phone unheard: *"I don't want to think about it, do you understand?"*

"There's also a car park at the other end of the lake," said Peter. "Who knows? There may be a payphone there. On some of my unauthorized outings from Meadowmeade I've discovered that the simple folk who live in these rural backwaters haven't yet learnt how to vandalize the public phones, and that some of the phones are still working and—get this—accepting coins!"

Peter rattled the change in his pocket to show Dunbar that he was well prepared to take advantage of such an opportunity.

"Good," said Dunbar. "The phone or the pass, I'm ready either way. We're going to make this thing happen."

He strode forward, as if trampling his doubts underfoot. There was something terse in his tone that brought the conversation to a close. The two men walked on in silence beside the lake. No longer facing the wind, Dunbar could see through the trunks and branches that this more sheltered shore was not splashed by ragged waves like the one in front of the hotel, but shivered with the interlocking ripples that radiated from the turbulent water farther out. The view from the path suddenly opened up, making him stop, almost involuntarily, in front of a black and silver beach on which a few large rocks were distributed with the perfect naturalness of a Japanese garden. Across the lake, a bare bronze mountain, with streaks of snow on its upper slopes, was marbled by a rapid flow of cloud shadows. How could this little island, whose pretty countryside he had mainly seen through the windows of speeding cars, returning to London from a conference in the Home Counties, or a weekend at Chequers, or a surprisingly rural estate in Buckinghamshire, suddenly generate such a ravishing and alien wilderness? With some difficulty, noticing that his mind was glazing over and getting lost in the luminous cross-hatching on the surface of the trembling water, he pulled himself away from the clearing and returned to the woodland path, to the therapeutic rhythm of the walk. Marching forward, he felt his anxiety abating enough to make room for his longing to see Florence again. This emotion, like the anxiety, was almost overwhelming, but not as vibrantly unpleasant. His yearning for reconciliation was so intense that if she had been there now he would have fallen to his knees to beg for her forgiveness. Why was he in this state? Or perhaps the question was why had he not always been in this state? Why had he not always found life so disturbing and so poignant? He spent the next half-hour preoccupied with the question of whether he was finally in a natural state or had, on the contrary, fallen away from his true nature. He couldn't reach any conclusion before Peter interrupted his reflections.

"I sure could use a drink."

"You've had a fair amount already," said Dunbar sternly.

"A fair amount," Peter protested, "what kind of a standard is that? I want to be taken to the International Court of Justice in The Hague to be put on trial for the unfair amount of drinking I've done."

"Is that the car park?" asked Dunbar, seeing an open space through the trees.

"The car park! Yes!" said Peter, reanimated. "I'll run ahead and hunt for a phone."

"Wait!" cried Dunbar, but Peter dashed off down the path.

When Dunbar found him again, Peter was standing next to the Information Center in the empty car park, dejected.

"It's broken," he said.

"We'll have to go over the pass then," said Dunbar, leaving no pause for self-pity.

"I'm not sure I can make it, old man," said Peter. "It's a climb and there'll be snow and it's quite a trek to Nutting, look at the map. I think we should go back to the King's Head."

He pointed out the trail to Dunbar on a brochure from the Information Center.

"It's a five-hour walk," said Peter, "it'll be dark before we get there."

"I've got a torch and a Swiss Army knife," said Dunbar.

"You certainly love all things Swiss," said Peter. "But to be honest with you, I can't go that long without a drink. I'll get a taxi and pick you up in Nutting."

"No you won't, they'll catch you if you go back."

"But you don't understand."

"Of course I understand, I've met plenty of drunks in my time," said Dunbar. "You must do what you have to, but I think you're making a mistake. Anyhow," he said, pulling a woollen cap out of his pocket and fitting it onto his head, "thanks for getting me out of that place; I couldn't have done it without you. By the way, you can keep the money you took from me, it'll give you a better chance of staying a step ahead of them."

"You're a good guy, Henry Dunbar, much better than I expected," said Peter, giving the old man a hug and slapping him rather too vigorously on the back.

Dunbar turned his collar up and, without another word, set off toward the trail at the other end of the car park.

6

Forced to restrain themselves in front of the staff on the plane, Abigail and Megan had checked in to the Royal Suite of one of Manchester's finest hotels and invited Dr. Bob to join them there for lunch. He was encouraged to defy the dangers of the important phone call he was about to make by the knowledge that the sisters would require ever-escalating doses of perversion to stimulate their jaded appetites. His body, already flecked with fiery welts and cuts, yellowing bruises, and, most recently, the thin row of renewed stitches in his chest, was screaming for revenge, while his conscience, struggling a little with the betrayal of his former patient, saw a kind of twisted retribution in going on to betray Dunbar's daughters as well.

After hanging the Do Not Disturb sign on his door, which in this particular hotel read, "I think I want some Me Time," Dr. Bob settled down at his desk, and got out his pre-paid cell phone, knowing that his own phone had been hacked by one of Abigail's keen assistants. He had memorized Steve Cogniccenti's special number so as to leave no record of his access to the charismatic and self-publicizing president of United Communications. Unicom, as everyone called it, was the only media organization larger than the Dunbar Trust. Separated by just two blocks, the New York headquarters of the two companies famously reflected each other in the darkened upper windows of their respective towers on Sixth Avenue. Their studios in Hollywood reiterated that uncomfortable proximity, but despite Unicom and the Dunbar Trust having chased the same prey for years, fighting over television stations, movie stars, and collapsing local newspapers, neither had ever dared to turn against the other directly, knowing that the failure of a takeover bid would carry too high a risk of self-destruction.

Eight on a Sunday morning would have been too early to call most people, but Steve had personally told Dr. Bob what millions of readers of the *Wall Street Journal*, the *Financial Times*, and *Fortune* magazine already knew: at this time on a Sunday, Cogniccenti would be coming to the end of an especially extended exercise routine, dictating emails and memos, while the Bloomberg business news streamed across the bottom of the virtual 3D Tour de France on the screen in front of his exercise bicycle. During this time he took calls from the happy few who were in possession of one of his private numbers, as well as beginning to place calls of his own around the waking world. His directives to the top executives and editors of Unicom followed the passage of the sun. Imperious Asian afternoons flowed into imperious European mornings and as the glistening orb passed over Manhattan, East Coast brags turned into West Coast visions; the assets stripped in one conversation became the potential maximized in another. Sometimes, on his way to dinner, just for the hell of it, he would put through a second call to his Asian staff and interrupt their yoga exercises or their first cup of coffee in order to chastise them for having achieved nothing overnight.

"Bob!" said Steve, as if he were greeting his best friend after a painfully long separation.

"Is this a good time?" asked Dr. Bob.

"Good? It's great!" said Steve, who benefited from sleeping with a pair of earplugs that artfully doubled as headphones, whispering affirmative messages into his sealed ears, just below the consciously audible level but guaranteed by the manufacturers to give their customers a subliminal injection of invincibility and unlimited entitlement. "Give your self-esteem a workout while you sleep . . . You deserve the greatest rewards that life has to offer." He had been skeptical when he first read the propaganda on his latest wife's latest Christmas present, but now it was hard to imagine spending a night without wearing his PowerSleep earplugs. Of nature's great mistakes, sleep had always struck him as the most outrageous, even harder to explain than altruism: three hours, or in the case of the truly lost, eight hours in which it was impossible to make any money. Even if investments flourished overnight, their success was based on old decisions;

nothing new, nothing audacious, nothing truly aggressive could be done in that jailhouse of obligatory passivity. At least with PowerSleep he knew that he was building himself a bulletproof ego for the Dodge City of perpetual competition and breaking news.

"What have you got for me?" said Steve.

"Well," said Dr. Bob, "I've confirmed that they can only go to a fifteen percent premium over the market price. Eagle Rock, their family fund, will launch its bid to take the Dunbar Trust private on Thursday morning, straight after the Board ratifies the offer."

"Only fifteen percent?"

A slight panting was audible between Steve's short sentences, forgivable in a man who was in one of the mountain sections of the Tour de France, cycling up a steep Pyrenean gradient. "I've gotta hear that meeting in real time. We'll use the microphone on your laptop."

"They may be able to go up another three percent," said Dr. Bob, "but that's the max. And one other thing: they want to remove Dunbar as non-executive chairman."

"What? They want to do this without his blessing? Their backers must be pretty confident."

"They've got Dick Bild organizing it."

"Victor's old partner," said Steve. "How close is he to Megan? He was basically her husband's only friend, right?"

"That's right, but I don't think the merry widow has him on her lovers' chain gang," said Dr. Bob.

"That may be a miscalculation," said Steve.

"Anyhow, they'll have me on the Board," said Dr. Bob, "and . . ."

"Well, I'm sure that's really fucking reassuring for them," said Steve, taking a hairpin bend on his virtual mountain road, "but you don't seem to get it, I'm paying for information here, I need something solid. What keeps them awake at night?"

"China," said Dr. Bob, dismayed by Steve's sudden change of tone.

"What, because they lost the satellite deal with Zhou? Unicom won the deal. Do you think I don't know about that? I organized it and it's all over the market that Dunbar is floundering in China."

"No, no, you don't understand. Zhou gave them some very impressive compensation. He doesn't want either of you bearing a grudge against China. The trading figures are amazing, and what keeps the girls awake at night is the idea that the good news will break out and the share price will rocket before they complete their deal."

"Now you're giving me something," said Steve. "And what are they doing with the old man?"

"Well, at the moment I'm in Manchester . . ."

"Manchester? What is this, 1850?" said Steve. "Why would anybody be in Manchester at this point?"

"Dunbar is in a sanatorium nearby," said Dr. Bob. "We want to move him to a more secure facility."

"The type you keep six foot underground," said Steve, with an immaculate laugh, neither too sinister nor too facetious. "No," he said, as if he was opposing someone else's misguided plan, "I'm fond of old Dunbar. He's built a great empire—which is why I'm going to have to take it over. But make the fuck sure you get him out of the picture, okay, Bob?"

"I will," said Dr. Bob, popping an Adderall with a little sip of water, to reinforce his conviction. "The only complication is his youngest daughter, Florence, who is also looking for him."

"What harm can she do us?"

"She might bring Dunbar back into play before the big meeting."

"So what's the plan?"

"We're going to take him to Austria, to a clinic with some serious security, unlike the genteel British place he's in at the moment."

"Isn't the company plane a little conspicuous?" said Steve, knowingly.

"That's why we're leaving Global One in Manchester as a kind of decoy and taking a rented jet out of Liverpool. Even if Florence finds her father's plane, it won't get her any closer to her father."

"Does she have any shares?"

"No, they got redistributed to the other daughters when she fell out with Dunbar."

"And she's the one looking for him? What is that? The loyalty of the maltreated—some kind of Stockholm syndrome?"

"That could be it, but in her case, I think she loves her father."

"You think she's a good person? That's your explanation? Do you have any idea how—"

"I'm sorry to interrupt, Steve, but I've just seen a
text from Abby on my other phone saying that she
needs to see me urgently."

"They've sure got you on a tight leash."

"You have no idea," said Dr. Bob.

"Hang in there, my friend! It's only till Thursday
night," said Steve.

Dr. Bob hung up the phone, knowing that if he
didn't turn up soon, Abby would be coming to get
him. His heart was pounding, his skin was stinging,
his mouth was parched, and his scalp was itching. He
was falling apart; he was just a body of uncontrollable
symptoms and raging side effects.

The long walk down the corridor to the Royal Suite
brought to mind his current bedside reading, a book
called *Cruel and Unusual Punishments*. The chapter
he had finished on the plane described how Jacobean
traitors, after an inconclusive hanging, were castrated
and disemboweled while still alive and then, perhaps
rather pedantically, torn apart. In his vulnerable state
of almost hysterical tiredness, in which the insides of
his eyelids seemed to be coated with sandpaper, the
polychrome chaos of the carpet underfoot, designed
to disguise stains by looking as if it had already suf-
fered every imaginable catastrophe before leaving the
factory, seemed to him like the boards of a scaffold
already spattered with the fruits of effusive torture.
Dr. Bob leant against the wall for a moment and let

out an involuntary sob. He was thinking about the execution of Sir Everard Digby, one of the men implicated in the Gunpowder Plot, who had managed, after his heart was ripped out and held aloft by the executioner with the cry, "This is the heart of a traitor," to gasp, "Thou liest!"

Dr. Bob was tempted to slide farther down the wall. Where was the pride of successful deception, the exhilaration of sudden advantage? Now more than ever he needed to connect with the cold-hearted bastard at the core of his being, but instead he was weeping over the defiance and integrity of a long-dead Catholic martyr, as if he were mourning something he could never have: the experience of sacrificing himself for a principle, a community, an ideal.

He punched the wall with a strangely autonomous violence, not emanating from his mood but imposed on it. In the absence of anyone else to be cruel to, he had to make do with his own knuckles. The pain shocked him out of his pitiful state of mind and as he straightened his body and resumed his progress down the corridor, he reminded himself that by Thursday evening he would be independently rich, not through the tedium of hard work, or through the depravity of a huge inheritance, but through his wit, his cunning, his charisma, and his transcendence of the slave morality that held lesser men in check. The combination of the payment Cogniccenti would be making into his Swiss bank account the next day and the expected doubling of the value of his Dunbar stock after the merger, as well as the salary he had wisely insisted on receiving from the Dunbar girls before he stabbed them in the back, would enable him to live what would be at least a simulacrum of the life he had grown used to as the entourage physician to billionaires. The income from his investments would still not be enough, but with no children and no intention of extending his life beyond his capacity to dominate the situations he found himself in, he was not averse to running through the capital and dying in debt.

By the time the double doors at the end of the corridor flew open, he had managed to introduce a certain swagger into his step.

"Where the hell have you been?" said Megan.

"No need to pump those bellows," said Dr. Bob, smiling as he approached, "you're burning with impatience already. You'd better watch out, or one day you might just," he paused and then snapped his fingers suddenly and loudly an inch from her eyes, "drop dead from a heart attack, or a stroke."

Megan looked startled and upset. How easy she was to dominate. These Dunbar girls were arrogant, imperious, and tough, but toughness was not strength, imperiousness was not authority, and their arrogance was an unearned pride born of an unearned income.

"Are you threatening me?" said Megan.

"Good God, no, who would ever be mad enough to do that?" said Dr. Bob, with a disarming chuckle. "I'm saying that you're a threat to yourself, if you live at this pitch of impatience. I'm your doctor, Meg, and I know it's not good for you to put yourself under this stress," he went on, resting an avuncular hand on her shoulder and reflecting that it would be wise not to show too much hostility and insubordination before the end of the week.

"Well, we've got a crisis on our hands, so I guess I'm not at my calmest," she conceded. "Daddy's escaped from that stupid sanatorium. Once we've got him back, we're going to sue them into the ground."

"I'm sure you are," said Dr. Bob, following her into the drawing room, but falling silent when he saw that Abigail was pacing the room, with her phone held to her ear.

"I warn you," said Abigail in response to what she had just heard, "we're going to be there by five o'clock this afternoon, and if my father isn't in his room when we arrive, you're going to read a series of articles about Meadowmeade that will redefine your idea of what bad publicity means."

She ended the call and threw her phone onto the sofa with a growl of frustration. Dr. Bob was skeptical about the threat she had just made. In all his years with Dunbar, although he had often seen the old man rant privately about destroying a reputation, he had never seen him make a direct threat. The threat should remain implicit but unmistakable. To expose it in a few angry sentences, as Abigail had done, was bound to make her look petty as well as entailing the fatal error of admitting that the news she sold was an instrument of her vindictive whims. The truth was that he had a duty to undermine her plans, if only to save half the world's media from being run on such capricious grounds. Although by the end of the week it might look as if he had contributed to the destruction of the Dunbar empire, he was in fact preserving it from further degradation, protecting it from its unworthy heirs. In the eyes of posterity he would probably be seen as its savior, but he shouldn't expect to get any thanks in the short term.

"Can you fucking believe it?" said Abigail. "Nobody has seen him since breakfast and they have no idea whether he's still on the property or not."

"He's strong for his age, but he can't have gone very far with no money and no phone," said Dr. Bob soothingly.

"He shouldn't have gone anywhere at all," said Abigail. "This was supposed to be a completely smooth and discreet operation."

"Which is why it would be better to hold back those ruthless articles about Meadowmeade losing your famous father."

"I was just keeping them on their toes," said Abigail.

"An empty threat is always a sign of weakness," said Dr. Bob.

"You can put away your kindergarten Machiavelli," said Abigail. "Remember who you are."

"And who we are," Megan added, delighted to gang up on the man who had just tried to terrorize her with his medical advice.

Dr. Bob was close to slapping them both or, worse, boasting about how wrong they were, in the light of his conversation with Steve Cogniccenti, but instead he managed to draw on his deep reserves of hypocrisy and recommit himself to a few more days of submission.

"I'm sorry. Of course you know more about handling power than I can ever hope to learn. It's in your DNA, as people like to say nowadays, however meaninglessly."

"We'll meet in the lobby in forty-five minutes," said Abby, turning her back on her chastened minion and walking away without another word.

"Great," said Dr. Bob, smiling this time without any dissimulation. There would be no time to go to bed; it was enough to make him believe in guardian angels.

7

Dunbar's path ran parallel to a stream that coursed down the middle of the hill. The white noise of rushing water helped to camouflage the anxious murmur of his thoughts. He treated each step and each breath as an individual package of concentration, pausing briefly when both his feet were safely on the ground and then starting up again. The climb ahead was steep and indistinct, but all he had to do was take the next step, propelled by the relentless forward motion that had characterized his entire adult life. He had always stretched into the future, bringing his business to new continents and bringing new technologies to his business, not because he understood them in any detail, or enjoyed using them himself, but because they smelt of novelty. Although he was still driven forward by these dogged habits, his confidence was now so easily destroyed that he was trying to reduce the horizon of anticipation, keeping his eyes on the ground immediately in front of him, as if darkness had already fallen and he was being guided by a lantern that only cast a faint pool of light a few yards ahead of him.

As he heard the splashing water grow closer, he allowed himself to glance up and saw that the path would soon be crossing the stream on an improvised bridge of flat stones. He lowered his head again and pressed on, but this time he found that the more resolutely he narrowed his field of vision, the more complexity seemed to emerge from it: the gray rocks on the edge of the path were covered in patches of white and acid green lichen, and where water gathered in cracks and hollows there were pockets of dark velvety moss. The broken rock on the path itself showed traces of rusty red and sometimes the momentary glitter of crystal. Like a child on a beach, he wanted to pick up the smooth stone with a white mineral vein encircling its dark surface, but he knew there would be no one to show it to.

By the time he reached the stream, he no longer felt protected by his downward gaze; on the contrary, it seemed to be drawing him into a vertigo of detail, a microscopic world that he didn't need a microscope to imagine, where every patch of lichen was a strangely colored forest of spores, their trunks rearing from the stony planet on which they lived. Freshly alarmed by how suggestible his mind had become, he decided to pause in the middle of the stream, needing to negotiate between the engulfing richness at his feet and accepting what until now had seemed to be the harder challenge of facing the scale of his isolation in such a wild and empty place.

He stood on the flat stones, facing downstream, imagining that the glassy water spilling over the gray rocks in front of him and tumbling into a foaming pool was also flowing through his troubled mind and washing away the confusion and dread that kept threatening to take it over. As it ran down the hill, the stream looked to him like an incision, a comparison that immediately gave him the mad feeling that a surgical knife was running down the center of his own torso. He moved his attention hurriedly on to the serene expanse of Merewater, but the sight of the now distant car park in which he had parted from Peter assailed him with a sense of bereavement that he didn't want to dwell on either. When at last he dared to look up he saw a canopy of thin broken cloud and, behind it, the detached blue of the upper sky flooded with light. The clouds themselves appeared to be racing toward him, funneled by the high hills on either side of the lake toward the pass at his back, making him feel trapped at the convergence point of a horizontal V. Along with this disturbing illusion, he felt an incoherent sense of guilt, as if the broken clouds were fragments of an infinitely precious blue and white vase he had been entrusted with and had stupidly dropped, and that he must somehow glue back together before the owner returned.

"Please don't let me go mad," he muttered, and then, after a pause, he tried to cover his secondary confusion. Who was he asking to grant him this mercy? He bowed to the stream with exaggerated courtesy, hoping that his sarcastic formality would give him some relief, but his need was too urgent to play with.

"Please, please, please, don't let me go mad," he begged, not making fun of anything anymore, and promising he never would again, if only this feeling would go away.

He twisted round desperately, trying not to lose his balance on the stones but wanting to get some idea of how much farther he had to climb to the pass. All the while he muttered, "please, please, please," hoping that his plea could imitate the fluency of the stream and, like the stream, flow into something greater and less agitated than itself.

The part of the hillside he stood on was already in shadow and although the pass was still sunlit, it was covered in snow. Some of the clouds were beginning to be stained by the sinking sun. As the light pushed its way through the polluted air closer to the ground, it shifted from the blue to the red end of the spectrum. That's all a sunset was: an exultation of dirt and dust. Perhaps his grandchildren would live under a perpetually red sky, as a dying nature, like an animal dangling upside down with its throat cut, bled into the firmament.

"Dirt and dust," Dunbar barked, relieved to find an external object of persecution, however briefly.

He crossed the stream, setting off at a faster pace, as if rapid movement might be able to peel away his terrifying thoughts. This presumptuous fantasy was immediately replaced by a sense of his own decrepitude, and then by the image of a man on fire who is trying to put out the flames by breaking into a run, but only succeeds in blazing more brightly. Nevertheless, he refused to give up, even under the relentless assault of his diseased imagination; he must get to the pass before dark, so as to see the shape of the next valley and get some idea of where he might find refuge for the night. The light was fading and the temperature falling but regardless of how he was feeling, he had to keep climbing, or he would die, he would really die—not just think he was dying, until Dr. Bob ran some tests to show that there was nothing fatal in the works, or paid a compliment to his constitution, or gave him a pill for his pillbox.

The thought of Dr. Bob forced Dunbar to pause, afraid that his heart could not stand the combination of such a fast climb and such breathless fury. His daughters, his flesh and blood and the man employed to minister to his flesh and blood, conspiring together. Betrayal was especially bitter since loyalty had always been one of the hallmarks of his astonishing ascent. Like Napoleon, who turned his sergeants into marshals, their mansions radiating from the Arc de Triomphe, he had taken Wilson and the rest of the original team with him as he rose from the provincial prosperity that came from inheriting the *Winnipeg Advertiser* to an unrivaled political influence in all the places that really mattered: the global power that was now being stolen from him by his daughters and his doctor, the diseases of his flesh and blood. How could he cure himself, except by opening his veins in this stream and letting out the disease with the blood? He felt the thick steel weight of the Swiss Army knife in his overcoat pocket and pictured himself kneeling in the stream, wisps of blood from his wrists curling and rushing down the hillside in the clear water. The animal slaughtered at sunset. The collision of ideas and images, the image of Catherine dead in a collision, the weird equivalence between what had really happened and what he had just imagined: they were all thoughts, all images fighting for control of his mind. It was not that past events, like Catherine's death, seemed unreal, but rather that every thought seemed so real. Perhaps that was why the universe was expanding: because thoughts were real and there were more and more people having more and more thoughts, drop after drop pushing the envelope of space farther and farther outward.

"Please, please, please . . ." he sobbed. "No more big ideas, please."

He wanted to sink to his knees, like a man in prayer, offsetting humiliation with humility, but he felt an even stronger desire to press forward, to move away from the disastrous frame of mind that now surrounded the ground on which he stood. If he knelt he would only sink more deeply into it, and so he set off again, glancing up from time to time to see where the intermittent shafts of sunlight were striking the snow-covered upper slopes. The light was now close to the summit and would soon overshoot the land altogether.

He could still remember the judgment of a journalist from a rival organization, it still throbbed in his forehead, like an old shrapnel wound, one of those stupid phrases purporting to summarize his career, not even elegant, but memorable for its injustice, "Cheap debt and plummeting standards." It was so wrong, so untrue. What about hard work and loyalty, not to mention coolness and courage and charm? Why was there no one to flatter and reassure him when he needed it most? He knew what it was to be surrounded by a halo of hollow praise, but now even Peter had abandoned him. He had quickly grown used to Peter distracting him, entertaining him, and looking after him. He had been an audience for Peter and Peter had been an audience for him, without either of them being able to listen to each other in the full, traditional sense of the word, due to the immense demands made by their own thoughts and impressions. Still, it was simply better to know that there was somebody there, that was all, somebody else—a relationship, that's probably what people would call it. There weren't many living things to have a relationship with up here; the crows knew better than to come up so high in the gathering darkness, and even the famously rugged Herdwick sheep, a dark, shaggy, local breed that Peter had become something of an expert on, after his many visits to Meadowmeade ("too numerous to innumerate," as he liked to say), hesitated to keep Dunbar company as he trudged toward the pass over the crunching snow.

As the ground flattened out, he came to a halt, arrested by an unexpected scene. The source of the stream, it turned out, was a small circular lake beneath the final ascent. Just to the left of the path, on the near side of the lake, was a perfect little beach, a natural resting place and contemplative opportunity, coated with snow. The water itself was covered in a thin, opaque sheet of ice, except where the pull of the stream kept it dark and liquid. A curved escarpment rose abruptly from the far shore, like a headdress on the brow of the lake. Dunbar found it piercingly beautiful, almost too beautiful, as if it had been choreographed for an exquisite death, a role that must have been reserved for him, since there was no one else for miles around. He hurried on superstitiously, like a pregnant woman who crosses herself as she realizes she is walking next to a cemetery wall, moving as fast as he dared over stones slippery with snow. The path circled the lake and then merged with the pass, which was now entirely in shadow. Only the very top of the mountain on the far side of the pass was still sometimes lit up with a splash of cold gold light.

There was nowhere, however lovely, that he couldn't contaminate with his morbid thoughts and his perpetual fear. He was being punished; there was no other explanation, punished for his own acts of treachery. What a hypocrite he was, raging against his daughters and his doctor. He had betrayed a wife he adored, keeping mistresses in all his major centers of operation, lying about the state of his marriage to encourage women who hesitated on the edge of adultery; he had treated Florence vindictively, cutting her off, rejecting her and persecuting her for having ideas of her own. His crimes were far worse than Megan's or Abigail's, let alone Dr. Bob's. He had betrayed the people he loved most, whereas his daughters presumably had the moral advantage of hating him, and poor Dr. Bob was just an opportunist who had seen an opportunity. In other circumstances, at a Sun Valley economic summit, or in conversation with a finance minister, he might have called it "enterprise" or "initiative." It was he, the enraged father and the indignant patient, who knew most about the twisted nature of betrayal, and now he had been dragged by a just fate to this sacrificial slab of rock and ice. There was no need for a feathered priest to tear his treacherous heart from his chest when it was ready to burst out from the pressure of its own guilt and grief.

Sick with fear and desperate to put the evil lake behind him, Dunbar stumbled into the deeper snow on the final ascent to the pass. No one had used the path since the last snowfall and he had no idea where it lay under the windblown drifts. All he could do was choose the most direct route, hoping that the snow would support him against the sharp stones and sudden hollows that he imagined hidden under every collapsing step. Although he had taken the precaution of tucking his trousers into his boots, the snow soon started to insinuate itself in a band around his ankles and to cling to his lower trouser legs. By the time he reached the top of the pass, he was frozen from the knee down, while his upper body was pouring with sweat, his heart pounding and his ears singing with the rush of blood.

As the bowl of the next valley opened up before him, he took in its emptiness, lightly criss-crossed with drystone walls, but without tree, or lake or any kind of refuge from the sky. Where was Nutting? Where was the signpost to Nutting? It was beginning to grow genuinely dark, although the snow retained an eerie luminosity. That final glow gave him scant re-assurance since he could only benefit from it by freez-ing to death. He turned around to have a last look at the valley he had been struggling across all day. He had tried to get away from it in the hope of finding some kind of safety; now, glancing back at the vil-lage and woodland car park, it looked like safety was what he was leaving behind. A bank of black cloud laden with rain and sleet and snow was replacing the broken, tinted cloud he had seen when he was strad-dling the stream lower down the hill. It was currently somewhere above the King's Head on the far side of the lake, but it was chasing after him and would soon be raining its cold vengeance on his poor old head. To return would be as profitless as to press forward, only shelter mattered now, but there was no shelter to be found.

8

Under different circumstances the four-poster bed, the leaded windowpanes, and the tiny roses tumbling down the wallpaper of her bedroom in the King's Head would have enchanted Megan. She was not alone among the brutal in cherishing her sentimental side. Dogs and horses had been spared her enthusiasm and dirndls left her cold, but she was helpless in the face of an English country house hotel. The King's Head was her idea of unpretentious heaven, right down to the card in the fireplace urging guests not to light a fire. It was all the better for being a make-believe fireplace in a country house hotel that had never been a country house. Sentimentality offered her a holiday from the harshness of the rest of her personality, a chance to kick off her shoes and wriggle her toes and watch something stupid on television, just like ordinary people, as she imagined them, a vast blur of undifferentiated banality beyond the ramparts of her own vicious and thrilling world.

It was all the more maddening, on this intemperate
Monday morning, with the rain pelting against the
leaden panes and the wind thudding and whistling in
the empty fireplace, and her father still missing, that
she was not able to enjoy a moment of cosy English-
ness before whisking him off to a secure facility among
the altogether more convincing mountains of Austria, mountains with jagged peaks, and glacial passes,
not these low, interlocking, round-backed mountains,
like a litter of sleeping puppies, into which it was evi-
dently all too easy to escape. Megan felt cheated of
a well-deserved treat. She decided to use her positive
visualization technique to bring about the outcome
she longed for: Daddy, after being sedated by Dr. Bob,
looking on in foolish admiration as she spread melting butter and strawberry jam on the cratered, lunar
surface of a well-toasted crumpet, while unspoilt Lake
District girls fell over themselves (and one another) to
bring extra clotted cream and finger sandwiches, their
own strawberry and cream complexions blushing uncontrollably at her appreciative glances, sensing what
she had in mind while being too innocent to be really
sure. Oh, God, it was so unfair! That selfish old man
was spoiling everything! Megan opened her eyes and
surged out of her chair. She couldn't afford to get too
worked up. Dr. Bob seemed to be on strike sexually,
and as far as she could tell the staff here consisted of
two bored Polish waiters, an Australian barman, and
a respectable female bookkeeper with short gray hair,
not quite the St. Trinian's meets Boucher tableau she
had just positively visualized.

The problem with men was that so few of them could play at her level and none could stay there. She liked a man to be totally in charge, in the wider context of being her slave, obviously, and only in order to facilitate her favorite role as a bewildered beginner, who looked up anxiously to ask, "Am I doing it right?" as she gripped him expertly with her hands or legs or mouth. She loved to whisper, "This is my first time," as she took up a position she had been in a thousand times before, with her legs nervously clenched. Given the chance, she would wince and gasp and bite her lip, as if she were being hurt by her big, rough assailant but didn't dare complain. The men who immediately got the boot were the ones who stopped at this point to ask if there was anything wrong; but those who thrived during the first week of repeated deflowering and faux initiations were taken deeper into the dungeon of her inversion of pain and love. In her view, pain was the gold standard to which the paper currency of love needed to be pegged. Pain could be measured, whereas love often couldn't even be located. Why not gradually exchange something that was not much better than a rumor for something real? Why not turn a fleeting emotion, always on the verge of reversing itself, into a repeatable sensation?

The place she was going to wipe off the face of the earth, when she could find a moment, was Meadowmeade. Dr. Harris and some ridiculous nurse, who was the last member of the staff to have seen Dunbar, had not been as obsequiously apologetic as she and Abby required. They had apologized of course, but without giving the impression that the Mariana Trench would be too shallow a grave for their shame and that, after finding Dunbar, they would both naturally be committing suicide as a small token of amends; in fact, after the third wave of daughterly indignation, Dr. Harris started to make remarks about not being part of the prison service, and Dunbar's medical condition having been misrepresented to him by Dr. Bob and his Hampstead colleague. In other words, he started to get uppity. She had sat in his office yesterday afternoon, staring at the paper-weight on his desk and imagining bringing it down on his smug English skull with "extreme prejudice," as people said in the movies when they were order-ing an official murder. The thick-ankled nurse then weighed in, saying that there was no need to "read us the Riot Act," that they were all well aware of the gravity of the situation, had already recaptured the two patients Dunbar had escaped with and had learnt from the one who was not already senile that Dun-bar had been trying to hitchhike his way to Cocker-mouth. As well as sending two members of staff to Cockermouth, she assured them that the local police were fully alerted and well aware of the need for dis-cretion. The thought of Daddy hitchhiking seemed to her an impossibly false note and she demanded to see the witness, who turned out to be the comedian Peter Walker. He made no attempt to disguise the nature of his difficulties.

"I've got a terrible alcohol problem," he said, sobbing wretchedly as he came into Dr. Harris's office, "I've run out of alcohol!" He slapped his thighs, wheezing with laughter. "The old ones are still the best," he said.

She and Abby insisted on taking him for a stroll around the grounds in order to hear his boisterous account of his adventures with Dunbar. They then did something rather naughty, luring him back to the King's Head, with promises of alcohol, so as to get him under their control and find out what had really happened. By the time they reached the Plumdale street corner where Walker claimed to have parted from Dunbar, adding the cunning detail that he *thought* he had seen him get into a silver Vauxhall Astra, it was beginning to grow dark and the storm that was still blustering outside had started to roll in. On a Sunday night in midwinter the King's Head turned out to have plenty of spare rooms and so they had taken the three best rooms for themselves and four "classic" rooms for the two bodyguards, the driver, and Peter, ignoring the texts and missed calls from Meadowmeade asking if they had any idea of his whereabouts.

Over dinner they gave Peter all the whisky he wanted, as well as a potion from Dr. Bob's medicine bag, which he definitely would not have wanted, if he'd been given any choice in the matter or had known what was in it. He started to drink even more rapidly to cope with the disinhibiting effects of a drug he didn't know he had taken. The more anxious he became, the more he became anxious to please.

"Those who know," he said, embarking unsteadily on his Jack Nicholson impersonation, "*know* that your father is *the man*—you know what I'm saying?"

"Not really," said Abby irritably.

"Given that he's *the man*," said Dr. Bob, intercepting Abby's hostility with an understanding smile, "we'd better find out where he is. If he's caught in this storm, he could be suffering terribly right now, and none of us wants that. You know what *I'm* saying?"

"I do," mumbled Peter, no longer certain that Dunbar's daughters were worse than the storm, and distraught about possibly putting his friend's life at risk.

"Because if you're not sure that you saw him get into that silver car," said Dr. Bob in a voice that couldn't reasonably be expected to carry any more warmth and empathy than it already did, "and you have any other ideas about where he might be, I would love to hear them, so we can reach out and make sure he's safe."

"I'm feeling really strange," said Peter with a directness none of them had seen before, "and I'm speaking as somebody—"

"Who really knows what he's talking about," Dr. Bob finished his sentence for him, with a peal of tuned-in, heartfelt laughter. "When it comes to strange, *you're the man*."

"I'm . . . I'm the man," said Peter, nervous of accepting the compliment.

"Would you like a Valium?" said Dr. Bob.

"Oh, yes, yes, yes," said Peter, "I would really like a Valium."

"Well, I can give you one, I'm a doctor!" said Dr. Bob. "I know you need to get a good night's sleep, 'sleep that knits up the raveled sleeve of care.'"

"Oh, I *need* to knit that raveled sleeve," said Peter, "I really do."

"I know what you're saying," said Dr. Bob, picking up the briefcase by his chair, "and I'm going to give you what you need, and if you can think of anywhere else we might look for Henry, just let me know."

"Nutting," mumbled Peter.

"Well, you're going to have to give us something if you want the Valium," said Abby angrily.

"I don't think he meant that," said Dr. Bob, repairing the damage with studied patience. "It's a place, isn't it?"

"Yes," said Peter, "Nut-ting."

Credit where credit was due: Dr. Bob had manipulated the hell out of Peter. Megan watched him at work with something approaching admiration—she didn't strictly speaking "do" admiration, which struck her as a desperate measure for desperate people, like selling your blood to a blood bank, not something that anyone as enviably placed as her was likely to be caught doing. Still, it was at these times of vague, approximate admiration that she most resented having to share Dr. Bob. She and Abby had always been passionately close and had always worked as a team, whether they were ganging up on a girl at boarding school, or planning which way to vote at an AGM, but now she wanted Dr. Bob to herself. She was the widow after all, and although Abby's marriage was a complete farce, she was not actually in a position to marry anyone. Sometimes, when Abby was literally driving her mad, Megan thought she would propose to Dr. Bob. In the end, though, she hesitated to turn her back on so many years of sibling collaboration. One absolute classic from the early years—she still marveled at how *organized* they had been at that age— was the case of an older girl at their boarding school who was known to have had an abortion during the summer holidays. She and Abby worked overtime to make sure that when the disappointed mother came back to school her room was stuffed with baby things: a beautiful old-fashioned cot with a mobile hanging over it, stacks of nappies, expensive creams, a breast milk extraction pump, piles of adorable little jump-suits, elaborately knitted cardigans, and every variety of soft toy peeping out from behind a cushion, or dangling its legs from the edge of a shelf; they had literally *emptied* the Slough branch of Mothercare. The pleasure of the practical joke was rather short-lived, since the girl, who invited persecution by being absurdly oversensitive, had an instant nervous breakdown, returning home immediately and never coming back. In assembly the next day the headmistress had promised to "get to the bottom" of "this appalling act of cruelty," but when she did get to the bottom of it and found two Dunbar girls there, she was subjected to an unexpected attack. Abigail said that they came from a very sheltered background and had never known about abortion until now. Yes, they had heard that one of the older girls was pregnant and had naturally thought that she would appreciate the presents they had bought for her. Perhaps it had been naive of them, but now that their innocent illusions had been shattered, what a pity it would be if the press got hold of the story and the school became known as "Abortion Abbey." Both sisters had gone on to be head girl, one after another, without their unforgettable reign ever being compromised by Florence, who was sent by her doting mother to an obvious day school in Manhattan.

It was bewildering, after witnessing such early masterpieces of sangfroid, to see Abby turn into the inept bully she had been last night. She did try to make up for it by dispatching Kevin, the head of security, and Jesus ("I prefer to be called J"), the handsome new bodyguard and former Green Beret who looked as if he could break your neck just by staring at you, into the storm in the middle of the night. When they arrived at Nutting, Kevin reported that it was hardly a place at all, with only four houses in it, a barn, and a red postbox built into a wall. He said there was no sign of Dunbar, but they would wait for first light to look for him along the footpath between Nutting and Plumdale, reversing the journey Peter claimed he was making. It had been light for three hours now and everyone was waiting to hear some news.

The lousy weather meant that they couldn't use a helicopter, and discretion ruled out the Merewater Mountain Rescue Association, a voluntary organization whose brochure Megan had seen in the hotel reception. With a helicopter they would have been sure to trap Dunbar, especially if it had thermal imaging. She had hunted by helicopter before—gazelle in Arabia, wild bull in New Zealand, hog in Texas—it was something that ostentatious people kept thrusting on her as a special kind of treat, but to be honest it was absolutely deadly being trapped in one of those swaying, shuddering machines, wearing headphones and a pair of goggles while spewing hundreds of empty shells a minute into the pristine countryside below. It made one feel like such a litterbug. The animals were rather pathetic as well, trying to escape the cacophony of flying metal by setting off on what might seem to them a virtuoso gallop, but from an aerial vantage point just looked like a bad choice made in slow motion. Baby hogs always dashed loyally after their mothers, so that if one killed or injured the mother, it was considered much kinder to finish off the baby as well, which meant circling back for another pass, grinning away as if one was having the time of one's life.

There was a knock on the door, interrupting Megan's reverie.

"Hello?"

"It's me," said Abby, "let me in."

Already dressed in jeans, a thick sweater, and boots, Abby pushed past Megan into the room and launched straight into the latest bulletin.

"Okay, so the boys have just called from some little lake above the main lake—I think that's what they said, but even their fancy satellite phones are challenged by this weather. Anyway, they've found nothing so far and it's snowing pretty hard up there, so that if there were tracks they'd be covered by now. I told them to come down on this side and meet us in the car park where Peter claims to have parted from Daddy. I thought we might take him there to refresh his memory."

"If he's been lying . . ." said Megan, not quite knowing how to describe what she had in mind.

"I know," said Abby. "In the meantime I've sent him a champagne breakfast in case he was thinking of taking his hangover back to Meadowmeade."

"Sweet," said Megan.

"I've got another treat in store for him later on."

"What?"

"You'll see," said Abby.

They agreed to meet downstairs as soon as possible. Abby had already told Dr. Bob to take charge of Peter.

Megan felt pleased to have her sister back: quick, decisive, mischievous Abby, a woman who knew how to have fun, not the short-tempered, inept, and slightly pompous figure she had become over the last few weeks. Naturally, they were both tense about taking over from Daddy, but if it wasn't going to be fun, what was the point?

As the car park was only a couple of miles away, Abby told George that she would do the driving. The real reason was that George was an old-timer they hadn't got rid of yet (there was so much to do!) and she and Abby were driven mad by his endless concerned questions about "Mr. Dunbar."

"But you'll need the second car if you're picking up the others," said George.

"Don't worry, we'll manage," said Abby, slamming the door. "They can walk if it means we don't have to sit in the car with you," she muttered to Megan through a clenched jaw.

"Bye," said Megan, waving through the window at the bewildered, windswept driver.

"Well, at least he's done something useful this morning," said Abby, smiling at Peter in the rearview mirror.

"What's that?" said Peter.

"Bought us a case of whisky."

"A case, a whole case?" said Peter. "Oh my, what have I done to deserve this undeserved good fortune?"

"You told us where to look for Daddy."

"Did you find him?" asked Peter. "Did you find Daddy?"

"Not yet," said Abby, "but we're going to go to the car park where the two of you parted, so that you can re-enact the scene with your amazing powers of recall and mimicry."

"Well, it was just like I said—"

"Just show us when we get there," Abby interrupted him.

They soon turned off the lakeside road into the deserted car park.

"I think I'm having a panic attack," said Peter to Dr. Bob. "Can I have another Valium?"

"I don't think that would be appropriate," said Dr. Bob, "the benzodiazepines are highly addictive."

"Okay, I admit I'm an addict! Now can I have one?

If it's not appropriate to give someone Valium during a panic attack, when is it appropriate?"

"There they are," said Dr. Bob to Abby, "in that little shelter next to the Information Center."

"There who are?" said Peter.

Abby drew up beside the shelter.

"Now that is appropriate," she said, "an information center, because what we want from you is some accurate information, Peter."

"But I've told you everything I know."

"Get out of the car."

"I can't get out of this car, I mean look at the weather; there are trees flying through the air *horizontally*— I wouldn't be surprised if this storm wasn't being filmed by one of the extreme weather channels . . ."

"Get out of the fucking car," shouted Abby. "We're talking about my father's survival here and it may depend on some detail you've forgotten to tell us. Now get out!"

Peter stumbled out of the car, blown sideways by the force of the wind.

"Steady there, Peter," said Kevin, putting an arm around his shoulder and guiding him into the shelter. "Bring the whisky," he said to Jesus.

"Oh, I see," said Peter, "it's party time! Why sit in the Lakeview Lounge of that depressingly comfortable hotel, sipping tiny cocktails, when you could be in a public car park, in sub-zero temperatures necking your very own bottle of Scotch? A man after my own heart."

"Sit down, Peter," said Kevin, "take the weight off. I know I could use a rest, but then I've been up since three in the morning looking for my employer's father. Two hours ago, I was up to my waist in snow, couldn't see shit, and do you know what I thought? I thought, if Peter's been giving us misleading information, I'm going to fucking crucify him!"

"But I didn't give you any misleading information," said Peter, "I promise."

"Hold his arms, J," said Kevin.

Peter's arms were twisted over the back of the bench and held in place by Jesus. Kevin unscrewed the tops from two bottles of whisky and started to pour them over Peter's head. The whisky soaked his hair, streamed down his face, and drenched his shirt and the lapels of his jacket. As soon as they were empty, Kevin replaced the bottles and got out two more full ones.

"What do you call this, son?" said US Colonel Peter, twisting his face up to suck in some of the second downpour, "Whisky-boarding? It should be mandatory under the Geneva Convention." Getting no response, Peter switched voices abruptly to a disgruntled customer, "I don't know how long you've been training as a barman, young man, but let me introduce you to a key concept: the glass, or any kind of container, a cocktail shaker, a coconut shell, or in your case a couple of big leaves stitched together with that surgical thread you use to sew up a wound after you've sucked a bullet out of your shoulder . . ."

Kevin went on impassively pouring bottle after

bottle of whisky over Peter's body, while Abby, Megan, and Dr. Bob took up positions around the shelter.

Peter transformed himself again, this time into a lisping Hispanic stylist. "Guys! I gotta tell you: this cocktail is not going to catch on. It's way too expensive, and it's crazy how messy it gets!"

"Shut the fuck up," said Kevin. "Unless you've got something to tell us about where we can find Mr. Dunbar, not another word."

"But I've told you," said Peter, beginning to sob.

"Do you know what this is?" said Abby, holding up a little silver pistol. She aimed it at her temple and pulled the trigger, producing a ferocious gas flame. "It's a Hurricane Lighter, designed to work in just these sorts of conditions."

"Mustn't forget the trousers," said Kevin, splashing more whisky into Peter's lap and onto his thighs and knees."

"No," said Peter. "No, no, no, no, please."

Abby sat down on the bench next to him, clicking the lighter on and off, like a nervous habit.

"So, you came here with my father yesterday," she said.

"It's like I told you," said Peter, who seemed to be having trouble breathing. "We parted over there . . . by the big tree . . . we shook hands . . . I told him there would be snow in the pass. You've got to believe me!"

Abby was too spellbound by the roaring cone of flame to listen to Peter. She brought the lighter closer to his face.

"I swear I'm telling the truth," sobbed Peter.

"I've seen a lot of men under interrogation," said Kevin, "and this one is telling the truth."

Abby let the lighter go out, just before running the hot barrel through Peter's whisky-soaked hair.

"Ouch!" Peter screamed. "You fucking burnt me! Your father is right: you're a monster, a fucking monster!"

"Really?" said Abby. "Is that what he says?" She calmly brought the pistol down to the level of Peter's navel and lit the edge of his shirt.

"Is that really necessary?" said Dr. Bob, wearily. "He's telling the truth now and he was already telling the truth last night, because he was psychologically prepared."

Peter had started screaming as a delicate blue flame spread slowly over his shirt and trousers.

"He needs to learn some manners," said Abby. "Nobody calls me a monster."

"It was a quotation. Let's find the man he was quoting. We've only got until Wednesday, at the latest, before we have to head back to New York. Let go of his arms, or we're going to have to take him to a fucking hospital."

Abby nodded her confirmation and J released Peter, who started frantically slapping out the flames on his chest and lap. He ran out of the shelter into the wind and the rain and soon put the fire out, but something in his mind seemed to have snapped and he continued to run toward the lake, gibbering and screaming.

"What a drama queen," said Abby.

"It's not like it was gasoline," said J. "What just went down could have happened in a fancy French restaurant."

"Collateral damage from a crêpe suzette," said Dr. Bob.

"That's right, sir," said J.

"Look, he's actually smoking," said Megan, "I've got to take a photo."

"I wouldn't do that, ma'am," said J respectfully.

"You're quite right," said Megan, clasping his muscular, tattooed forearm. "I was getting carried away."

They looked on as Peter waded into the lake, shouting incoherent curses at the sky. After a few yards he slipped on one of the unreliable stones underfoot, lost his balance, and toppled into the water.

This was too much for Abby and Megan, who got such contagious giggles that they had to lean on each other for support.

"At last I can see why people think he's funny," said Megan, applauding as Peter floundered around in the frigid water.

"I hate to spoil your fun," said Dr. Bob, looking up from his phone, "but I just got a message from Jim Sage. He says that Florence is flying in to Manchester and has asked him where you are."

"Just ignore it," said Abby, snapping into action. "If he doesn't know, he can't tell her, but we don't want to tell him not to tell her. Okay, let's go back to Nutting and start asking questions. Presumably you didn't go into those four houses in the middle of the night."

"No, we didn't want the attention," said Kevin.

"I'll go on foot, ma'am," said J. "That way if he tries to come back here, I can round him up."

"Good idea," said Abby.

"You're such a hero," said Megan, resting her hand back on J's arm. She was enthralled by the energy she could feel radiating from his body: here was a man who knew all about killing and all about fucking, and almost nothing about anything else. Absolute heaven.

"I'm just doing my job, ma'am," said J, hoisting his rucksack onto his back. "I'll see you all in Nutting."

"Look, darling," said Megan to Abby, "he's jogging!"

"As he says, he's just doing his job."

Megan watched J until he disappeared into the trees.

"Come on, come on," said Abby, drumming her fingers on the steering wheel.

Megan climbed into the back seat, next to Dr. Bob. She glanced back and saw Peter. She had completely forgotten about him, he seemed so irrelevant now. He was back on the shore in what a yoga teacher would have called child's pose, kneeling forward with his back arched and his forehead on his folded arms.

"Baptized by fire and baptized by water," said Dr. Bob. "If he's not born again, I don't know who is."

"*Don't,*" said Megan, "you're making me jealous."

9

Dunbar clambered over the stile as stealthily as he could and once he was crouching behind the drystone wall on the other side, looked back at the disappointing hamlet of Nutting and at the barn where he had spent part of the night. He was not certain whether he had been spotted by anyone, but until he got out of the bowl of this valley he was as conspicuous as an insect crawling across a windowpane. His plan had been to wait until morning to ask one of the residents to call him a taxi for London. He dreaded the prospect of this social exertion, fearing that he was in too much of a muddle to make himself understood. If he looked as mad as he felt, he was more likely to end up in an ambulance or a police car than a taxi. His muddle was at once immediate and fundamental; he seemed to be reaching for the keys of a piano that was sliding across the floor of a sinking ship, trying to remember snatches of a piece he had once known by heart.

Part of him was grateful not to face the challenge of a human encounter. He was driven to be alone with his madness, even if being alone was driving him increasingly mad. Perhaps there was a point at which the disorder would become a new kind of order, or at least a new kind of perspective, like a pilot who struggles through an overcast sky and then emerges from blindness into the serene light of the upper atmosphere, looking down on a sea of cloud beneath the wings, seeing completely what had just prevented him from seeing at all. Yes, that's what he wanted, that's what he desperately wanted.

He had been forced to leave Nutting in a hurry because of the two men who had come into the barn last night. He heard them whispering his name and knew that they were there to hunt him down. Luckily he had found a hollow between two bales of hay where he was hidden from the spying beams of their torches. The barn had cattle on one side, warming the atmosphere with their breath and their bodies, and bales of hay on the other. Opposite the entrance was a tractor smelling of oil and earth and wet metal. He had arrived a few hours before the two killers, turning on his own torch in brief, apprehensive bursts, much more aware of its light as a means of drawing unwanted attention to himself than as a means of locating the things he wanted. Eventually his flickering research revealed the pile of empty sacks in the corner next to the tractor, and the convenient hollow where he made his bed. He took off his overcoat, heavy with rain, and covered himself in dry sacking, spreading the overcoat back on top as a blanket, so that its weight and the warmth of its fur lining would help him to sleep, while the outer layer had a chance to dry. Under the circumstances it was a triumph of domesticity, but he was too hungry and too vigilant to fall into a deep sleep, and the moment the barn door opened, briefly amplifying the sound of the storm, he woke up with a pounding heart. He couldn't hear what they were saying at first, but when the door was closed again and they moved to the middle of the barn, directly under his hiding place, he heard every word through a gap in the bales.

"Dunbar wouldn't knock on a stranger's door in the middle of the night," said the first man, whose voice Dunbar knew he should recognize. "He likes to be in the driving seat, hates owing favors, and even if he is holed up in one of the houses, the way to handle that one is to come back in the morning, all concerned about an old geezer from our rambling club who got lost in the storm."

"My folks have got a barn on our farm in Texas, but it ain't anything like this," said the second man.

"That's so fucking interesting, J," said the first man. "Why don't we sit down while you tell me all about your parents' barn? I mean, that's why we came here, right?" He let out a hoot of derisive laughter. "Check out the cab of the tractor, he might have gone in there to sleep."

They moved around below him, looking in the tractor and under the tarpaulins that covered the trailers and plows.

Of course! He had worked it out. The English one

was Abigail's security man: whatshisname—Kevin, that was it, Kevin—the nasty Brit who had been in the Special Forces. All the bodyguards had been in the Special Forces and now they were going to use their special forces to destroy his mind, shattering it like a clay pigeon blasted out of the air. That's what they were expert at, keeping people physically alive for long enough to experience their own psychological destruction. Well, he wasn't going to let them take him alive. Maybe he could push one of the bales off the top of the stack and break Kevin's neck. Dunbar would go down fighting—as long as he could go on being Dunbar.

"There's no way that old fat cat could climb up a straw castle like that," said Kevin, "but why don't you nip up there all the same and have a look. I'll check out the beef."

"Those are hay bales and the cattle are dairy," said J, still harping on his rural background.

"Oh, really?" said Kevin. "What is this, the Royal fucking Agricultural College? You would have thought I knew enough about prize cows, given that I work for one, but I wouldn't want to pass over the opportunity to learn from a gen-u-ine fucking cowboy."

Dunbar's body was rigid with anxiety, listening to the creaking bales as J climbed toward him. His hiding place was about halfway along the top of the stack, not immediately visible, but easy enough to find.

Kevin approached the cattle scornfully, catching alarmed and glassy eyes in the powerful beam of his torch. Perhaps sensing his hostile attitude, the cattle grew restless and their restlessness grew contagious; one or two cows bellowed, while others barged against the clanging metal gates of the pen. Moments later a dog started to bark and then another.

Just as Dunbar heard J hoist himself onto the top of the stack, he also heard Kevin hiss at him from below.

"Get down here—the whole fucking farmyard is kicking off!"

J came down in a few easy jumps.

"Nothing up there anyhow," he said.

"Let's get the fuck out of here before Old MacDonald turns up with his shotgun," said Kevin.

The two men slipped out of the barn, leaving Dunbar in a state of beatific relief. He couldn't remember ever being so happy. The cattle had protected him and the dogs had protected him, as they had earlier, after he crossed the pass, when he was stumbling around below the snowline, tormented by sleet on the dark and featureless slope, and he had heard the faint sound of a barking dog, answered by another (just like now) and then a human voice encouraging the dogs to come inside, or to stop barking; the words were inaudible, but the tone was one of coaxing command rather than anger. That series of sounds had drawn him in the right direction until he saw the light that turned out to be shining onto the yard in front of the barn. And now, at another point of crisis, the animals had intervened a second time, making him realize with a rush of joy that nature was supporting him, conspiring with him in shared indignation against the unnatural cruelty of his older daughters.

He had always had a strong connection with nature, spending the summers of his youth in the holiday house he thought of as his true home, in the Ontario woods next to a lake that he still owned, canoeing, sailing, working on his tree house, hiking, camping, drinking the cool water of the lake as he swam through it, feeling effortlessly connected to the plants and trees and animals around him. Age and money had alienated him from that relationship, but now that he was being tested to the limit, he was also being restored to a deeper instinct, an older identity. How wrong Kevin was to think that he was "an old fat cat" who couldn't climb the haystack in which he had successfully hidden while his persecutors floundered around the barn. He had always had a prodigious amount of raw physical energy. He needed no more than three hours' sleep to function perfectly for the rest of the day. That muscle-bound moron had no idea who he was dealing with; he was too fascinated by his own fitness and belligerence to find out what inner strength really was.

Within a few minutes Dunbar's elation had peaked and dissipated and disappeared. He started to wonder if Kevin and his murderous apprentice had really left, or were in fact hiding a few yards away, their telescopic lenses focused on the barn door? Was the heavily armed MacDonald on his way to find out what had disturbed his guard dogs and his cattle? He must find a way out before it was too late. Only the front yard was lit up; if the tall sliding door behind the tractor was unlocked and he had the strength to open it, he should be able to leave undetected. He climbed down from the haystack, the tight string on the bales cutting into his fingers as he searched for his next foothold. When he got to the back door he summoned all his strength to push the lever to one side, only to find that the door sprung open and almost dragged him along its smooth rails. He slipped through the opening and closed the door behind him. Although the weather was still foul, it was no longer completely dark and so Dunbar turned up his collar and pulled down his cap and headed immediately in the direction that would take him still farther from his last known location in the King's Head or, if Peter had blabbed, in the car park.

And now, after a steady climb, he was crouching behind the drystone wall, only three fields away from the top of the hill, looking back at the hamlet and the barn. It had grown light enough to see his way clearly, but also to be seen clearly by his enemies. There was a black Land Rover parked two hundred yards before the last turning to Nutting. It was facing the opposite direction to his climb, and nobody inside it would have been able to see him except through the back window, but its presence weighed on Dunbar's mind much more than the houses and the other cars parked around them. As he prevaricated behind the wall, he saw the doors of the Land Rover open and watched as two men got out, took their rucksacks from the back seats and hoisted them onto their shoulders. They set off at a military pace in the direction of the Merewater footpath. He couldn't make out their faces, but he was certain that it was Kevin and J, starting out on their hunt.

He squatted down, his back pressed to the wall, shocked by how close he had come to being caught. Now he would have to wait until they had gone through the pass, otherwise they would turn around at any point and see him on the other side of the valley. His heart was racing from the panic of knowing that had they set off a minute earlier, they could have looked up and seen him climbing over the stile. Whereas his previous reprieve had filled him with a sense of gratitude and destiny and the beneficence of nature, this second piece of good fortune sent him the other way, deepening his underlying sense of horror, feeling like a man being slowly drowned by ferocious surf, occasionally glimpsing the Pacific beach he should never have left, as he is dragged down deeper and longer with each wave. On top of feeling generally disoriented all the time, like someone who has forgotten how to tie his shoelaces or to name the familiar objects around him, he was also being subjected to spasms of much deeper perplexity. Right now, he felt a root confusion, as if he had just witnessed something impossible, a reversal of the laws of nature, like a stone being thrown into the air, which instead of falling downward, continues to accelerate into the sky.

The ground was hard and wet, but it was only a few feet away; it was his friend. He longed to fall to the ground, if it meant that he didn't have to fall indefinitely into the sky—with his eyes closed and his mind twisting backward toward the home he had lost.

Dunbar lay down at the foot of the wall, and spread himself out so that as much of his body as possible was touching the earth. He didn't want to be taken away. Searching blindly for extra anchorage, his right hand wrapped itself around a stone protruding from the wall, grazing his fingers against its rough surface, while he gripped a tuft of grass with his other hand. He was reminded of desperately clinging to table legs when he was little to prevent his mother from dragging him away for punishment. One time he was beaten for lighting a fire he had "specifically" been told not to touch. He was haunted by that word long before he knew what it meant. He assumed that it conveyed a dreadful moral weight, referring to something for which "evil" was no longer adequate. When he learnt its real meaning, the neutrality of its precision bewildered him. How could she hope to load so much terror and violence onto such a prim, narrow word?

"Specifically," muttered Dunbar.

He continued to sprawl in the mud, clinging onto the ground by tuft and stone, with his toes dug in and his muscles rigid, not daring to let go. He couldn't have said how long he stayed there. His sense of time was as warped as everything else, it had the intimate authority of a nightmare: he couldn't judge how long he was lost in the atmosphere of his mother's punitive rages: it seemed to be outside time because the experience, although it was over, belonged to a time when he couldn't imagine it ending. On the other hand, concepts like infinity and space flashed across his mind in a fraction of a second, but left him infused with the hellish promise of eternal punishment.

When he eventually moved, he rose slowly to his aching knees and then onto his numb feet. He kept his head below the top of the wall in case his pursuers were looking across the valley with powerful binoculars. After a further pause, he glanced furtively over the wall to see how far they had climbed. There was no one there. He traced the line from their car up toward the pass, but could only see bedraggled black sheep lashed by wind-twisted ropes of rain. Perhaps his pursuers had already disappeared into the clouds that obscured the upper slopes. It scarcely seemed possible. How long had he been hiding? Were they already on their way back? Should he go back to Nutting and simply give himself up, ask for the police rather than a taxi, since it was the police they would call anyway? Should he ask to be taken back to Meadowmeade and put back on his meds?

No, he would not go back down the hill. He would not debase himself; he would not be ruled by his children and insulted by his jailers. Hunger could digest his stomach and frost shatter his blood before he would bow down. He forced himself to start walking again. His pursuers were gone for the moment and he must get as far ahead of them as he could. Like a pack of hounds distracted by a false trail, they were panting their way over the pass to Merewater, but they were moving so fast that when they found nothing on the other side they would be back, yelping and barking and pouring over fences, driving him farther and farther into the hills, like a stag with burning lungs and trembling limbs, splashing through rivers, hoping to put them off the scent, only to get trapped in a thicket or a pond, hounded to exhaustion. He had seen the whole thing in the Loire valley once. They fed the entrails to the dogs as a reward for not dismembering the cornered stag, for having the discipline to leave the Master of the Hunt the pleasure of piercing that wild animal through the heart.

10

None of them, it turned out, had been to Manchester before, except Wilson, who explained to Florence that he had been there with her father to buy a television station.

"What did you do with it?" asked Florence.

"We shut it down," said Wilson.

"Was that the alluring business plan you seduced them with?"

"Not exactly," said Wilson, smiling at her. They had been discussing Florence's misgivings about her father's empire ever since her embattled adolescence, when she turned into a passionate advocate of workers' rights, environmental concerns, and high standards of journalistic integrity.

Florence smiled back; Wilson was part of the family, or rather, to his infinite credit, he was *not* part of the family, but was someone she had known all her life and loved for his loyalty and good humor.

"I feel so guilty about renting this private jet," she

said. "I only just finished persuading my kids that it's an immoral practice because of the carbon footprint."

"Well," said Wilson, "sometimes you have to buy a TV station to destroy the competition, and sometimes you have to rent a jet to catch up with the competition—in this case your sisters."

"And then we had a last-minute passenger," said Florence, rounding her eyes with surprise, but not wanting to say too much.

"That's right," said Wilson, also ruled by tact. "Well, I think we should make use of some of those carbon beds you've rented for us, so we arrive in Manchester in reasonable shape. It's not that long a flight."

"I planted seventy thousand trees last year," said Florence.

"And now it's time to give them some airborne fertilizer," said Wilson, resting a hand on her shoulder. "Goodnight, Flo, I'll see you in the Northern Powerhouse."

"Goodnight," said Florence, placing her hand briefly on top of his in a gesture of tired farewell.

She soon retreated to the soundproofed compactness of her own bedroom, kicking off her shoes, peeling off her dress, replacing her bra with a T-shirt, brushing her teeth in a trance of pure routine, and sinking onto the bed. She worked her body under the sheets, put in her earplugs, strapped on her eyeshades, and then lifted them up again to switch off the light.

The unexpected passenger she had been reluctant to discuss, in case he was in earshot, was Mark. He had called her back while Wilson and Chris were still on their flight from Vancouver and said that he wanted to help find his father-in-law. Florence was not sure what to make of his change of heart, only a few hours after he had chosen his own safety over any other consideration, but she felt intuitively that she was dealing with a kind of brittle sincerity. His hatred of Abigail, although intense, stumbled convincingly under the weight of conflict and guilt. If Wilson was completely opposed to his participation, she could still cancel Mark's invitation, but in the meantime she thought they might as well all converge on LaGuardia airport.

"Let your friends wander, but hold your enemies close," had been Wilson's cryptic response when she told him about Mark.

"What's that from, *The Godfather* or *The Art of War*?" asked Florence.

"I don't know," said Wilson, "I just made it up."

"Wilson! I need some serious advice."

"Listen, we don't really have a plan, so Mark can't betray us by telling your sisters what our plan is; on the other hand, he might tell *us* something useful. On balance, I think he should come along."

Once they knew that Dunbar was imprisoned somewhere in the northwest of England, Wilson's team of researchers had come up with three plausible private clinics to investigate, but none of the receptionists would confirm that he was among their patients and there seemed to be no way of knowing whether it was secrecy, ignorance, or absence that made him impossible to find. By the time Wilson arrived at LaGuardia, one of his interns was confident enough to suggest that they could bring the number of clinics down to two, unless the night porter she had spoken to was "about to win an Oscar" for his incredulous response, which she impersonated for Wilson in a hopeless parody of an English accent that made Dick Van Dyke's chimney sweep sound like a cockney born and bred.

"What? *The* Hen-e-ry Dunbar? The famous Hen-e-ry Dunbar? We 'aven't got him 'ere, love, or I'd know about it. You couldn't keep a secret like that in this place."

Florence and Wilson were won over by this reported indiscretion, and decided (without telling Mark) to divide into two teams the next morning, each checking out one of the remaining candidates.

"I'll go with Chris," said Florence. "You'll be better at working out what Mark's motives are. Anyway," she added, with one of those sudden collapses into directness that Wilson had always loved her for, "I want to go with Chris."

"Sure," said Wilson, playing along with the practicality of her suggestion, while thinking of the time when he and Dunbar used to discuss whether their children were going to marry each other. "I'd like the chance to see if I can find out why your sisters were quite so pleased to see me leave the Board. Mark may not even know what he knows—there may be some details that will give me a sense of where they're headed."

If Florence was now having trouble getting to

sleep—and she was—it was partly from the prospect of being alone with Chris, driving through the reputedly ravishing Lake District, looking for a place called Meadowmeade. Neither of them had ever visited the Lake District before and despite the urgent and ominous nature of their journey, Florence couldn't help thinking of the many excursions they had been on over the years, especially the years when they were going out together in their early twenties. Inconveniently, her most persistent memories and reimaginings of sexual passion belonged to her time with Chris. Right at the beginning there had been raw obsession; dressing was a tedious preliminary to undressing; they couldn't make it through a party without eloping to the back seat of their car, returning glazed and disheveled to the near irrelevance, the elevator music of other people. When she was twenty-three they went on a tour of Europe and she could remember thinking that it must be impossible to feel more complete, staring out from their bedroom at the red-brick tower of San Giorgio, as it appeared and disappeared, while the thin white curtains bellied out in the breeze from the lagoon and sank back languidly into the frame of the French windows. She still daydreamed about the time they had trekked in New Mexico and found a pale ocher cave where the ground was so smooth and the dust so warm and soft and thick that it was impossible to find an uncomfortable position, although goodness knows they had tried, kneeling and twisting and rolling in the dirt. Oh, God, it was so long ago but still closer than anything else, at least at the moment,

on this small plane, with only a flimsy partition between their rooms.

It was out of the question to be unfaithful to Ben, or
at any rate it had been so far. Was adultery with someone who had a claim older than the marriage worse
than standard adultery, or was it just the restoration
of a natural order that the marriage had interrupted?
How could she even be asking? She loved Benjamin
as a husband, as someone she had made children
with. She had been dedicated to avoiding pregnancy
with all her other lovers, all except Chris. The two of
them had lived in an intermediate zone: too young
and volatile to form a clear intention, too reckless and
passionate not to expect an accident. In a sense the
accident was that she didn't get pregnant with Chris.
By the time she could formulate her regret, they had
definitively separated, as opposed to storming out of
each other's apartments, as they did every few weeks
when they were going out.

There was something faintly incestuous about the
depth of her relationship with Chris. Her father had
taken to his role as godfather enthusiastically and
Chris had always been around during her childhood,
spending a good part of the long summer holidays
with the Dunbars at Home Lake. Despite the clashing
teeth and colliding noses of their first late childhood
kiss, Chris could easily have fallen into a brotherly
role, or at least become too familiar to be alluring, if it
hadn't been for the crucial years in which they hardly
saw each other, during the time that Wilson was in
charge of the company's European headquarters.

Chris was sent to boarding school in England and started spending his summers in Italy and France. Although Dunbar continued to see his godson on his frequent trips to Europe, Florence missed the first half of his adolescence. Meeting him again when they were both seventeen, she had the strange thrill of feeling shy in front of someone she was used to thinking she knew all about; it was like discovering that the house she lived in had another wing she had somehow failed to notice but now longed to move into. Neither of them knew what to do with this confluence of contradictory currents. When, much later, they saw the "Meeting of the Waters" in Manaus, where the sluggish, yellow Amazon and the swift, cool Rio Negro run parallel for several miles without mingling, she had compared it to that summer, when her old, easy, fond feeling for Chris was joined by a new, sharp sense of desire and for a long time she could find no way to integrate them. It was only the following Christmas that they had started kissing for hours on end, and only the next summer that they made love for the first time. Florence was rather shocked to find herself thinking that in the face of such a primal connection, it was really her marriage that was the adulterous act. She must get some sleep now. As someone who almost never took a pill, she benefited fully from the impact of the Xanax she shook from its five-year-old tub and was very soon unconscious.

The sound of knocking barely reached her down the well of her artificial sleep, but when the stewardess tentatively opened the door to say that they were coming in to land, Florence was able to thank her and ask if she could have a double macchiato along with her usual pot of green tea. She groped her way into her clothes, gulped down her coffee, fastened her seatbelt, and was soon dozing again in a stupendous leather seat.

The weather in Manchester was foul, but from under the umbrella held for her by the driver Florence took a detached pleasure in the shivering puddles and the stray, refreshing drops of rain blown into her face as she crossed the tarmac to climb into the high back seat of a Range Rover. Chris got in beside her and, as if the fifteen years since they were together had been abolished, she mumbled, "I really need to get some more sleep," and sank sideways onto him, resting her head in his lap. Chris welcomed this unexpected burden, wrapping an arm tenderly around her waist to protect her from being thrown forward in case the car stopped too abruptly.

For the first few moments after she woke up, Florence had no idea where she was at all. When she worked out that her head was in Chris's lap, she tried to be alarmed, but soon resigned herself to how sweet and natural it was to be there.

"I'm sorry, I must have fallen asleep," she said, heaving herself up.

"You sort of asked permission," said Chris.

"So, you're not going to sue me for violating your personal space and causing you mental anguish and loss of self-esteem?"

"Not this time," said Chris, "but we ought to draw up a contract and get it witnessed."

Florence squeezed his hand briefly but said nothing, feeling that it would be too provocative but also too superficial to banter with him.

"Where exactly are we?" she asked the driver.

"According to my satnav," said the driver, preparing to serve her word back to her, "we are *exactly* nine point six miles from our destination."

"That sounds awfully close for someone who was in Wyoming thirty-six hours ago."

"I should say that you've done *roughly* ninety-nine point eight percent of your journey," said Chris.

"Only if he turns out to be there."

Dr. Harris told them that he was in no mood to joke.

"Surely your sisters have already told you what has happened."

"They have told me nothing," said Florence. "We don't communicate."

"Well, I'm sorry to say that they've been communicating all too much with me," said Dr. Harris. "Yesterday, I had the honor of being insulted by them personally, but today they have handed over that task to some extremely aggressive solicitors in London."

"Braggs?" asked Florence.

"Yes."

"I may be able to put a stop to that," she said.

"Well, in any case," said Dr. Harris, refusing to be appeased, "two can play at that game. My failure to run a high security prison, which I have never offered to do, is going to look like a minor infraction compared to kidnapping one of my patients and, by his account, torturing him to extract information about Dunbar. When we found him an hour ago in Plumdale, he was in a state of abject terror. We've had to sedate him and put him in a Suicide Observation Room. Let's see how *that* looks in court."

"Torturing?" said Florence. "Can I talk to him?"

"What, so you can set light to him as well? I think he's had quite enough contact with your family to last him a lifetime."

"I am not my family," said Florence.

"Well, I'll be pondering the profundity of that remark for the rest of the day, I'm sure," said Dr. Harris. "Nevertheless, if you ever feel the need for a private sanatorium, please apply *elsewhere*."

"Dr. Harris, slow down," said Chris.

"I want to make it clear," said Dr. Harris, rising from his chair and leaning across his desk toward his two visitors, "that I will not be bullied by your sisters or their representatives. I deeply regret your father's disappearance, but not as much as I regret accepting him here in the first place. Celebrities are usually more trouble than they're worth, but in the case of your father, who is also an immensely powerful man, his presence here has been a complete disaster."

"What have you been doing to find him?" said Chris.

"We're doing everything in our power," said Dr. Harris, straightening up and folding his arms across his chest, "and were about to involve the police and mountain rescue when his daughters, his two *other* daughters," he specified, "decided to take charge of everything themselves. I will not be held responsible for the consequences."

"We're not interested in blame, just in getting Henry Dunbar to a safe place," said Chris. "The reason he's exposed himself to a storm in this mountainous country is that Abigail and Megan are more of a threat to him than lightning and frost and hypothermia. I've known him all my life and I know that he would have to lose himself entirely before he lost his tenacity and his instinct for power. Those are the things that have made him great."

"Unfortunately, people do lose themselves entirely," said Dr. Harris, responding to Chris's conciliatory tone with a calmer tone of his own, "we see it every day. Dunbar, although he was often deluded and extremely choleric, was certainly not worn down to that degree. All we know about his disappearance is that he was last seen yesterday afternoon in a car park on the shores of Merewater, heading toward a place called Nutting."

Dr. Harris walked over to an Ordnance Survey map on the wall of his office and pointed out to Florence the journey that Dunbar was supposed to have made. Chris stayed seated, texting on his phone.

"It would be a hard walk for anyone at this time of year, let alone for an eighty-year-old man. At least the storm is dying down."

"That's good," said Florence, "but in any case, as Chris has said, my father is the most determined, not to say the most stubborn man you're ever likely to meet."

"Okay," said Chris, looking up from his phone, "we're meeting my father in Nutting in half an hour and he's going to get in touch with the police and the mountain rescue, and help deflect the killer emails from Braggs."

"But I thought he was checking out the other clinic, the one on the far side of Manchester," said Florence.

"I told him the moment we found out this was the right place," said Chris. "He's already on his way."

"Not Temple Grove?" Dr. Harris couldn't help asking. "Dreadful place; I hope you're not thinking of sending anyone there."

"We're not thinking of sending my father anywhere," said Florence, "we're thinking of taking him home."

"Well, I guess we'd better head off," said Chris, shaking hands with Dr. Harris.

"Let me know how your patient is doing," said Florence, "the one in the Suicide Observation Room. I'm horrified by what you've told me and want to do anything I can to help."

"I will," said Dr. Harris. "I'm sorry I mistook you for the third wave of an apparently relentless attack," he added.

"A natural assumption after what you've been through," said Chris, smiling firmly.

"You've become so efficient," said Florence as their car drew away from Meadowmeade. "I remember when you were . . ."

"Totally chaotic," said Chris.

"Well, yes," she laughed.

"I think we got across the idea that Henry is a stubborn guy," said Chris as cheerfully as he could.

"Let's hope he's stubborn enough," said Florence. She stared out of the window, not wanting to let Chris see that she was crying, and not knowing precisely what combination of emotions was making her cry. She reached blindly for his hand and raised it to her lips to kiss.

"Oh, he's stubborn enough," said Chris, reversing the grip of their entwined fingers and bringing her hand to his lips.

11

Dunbar tried to shake off the latest scrap of disjointed narrative that had taken over his mind like a hallucination, but he had been alone for too long and was now adrift in a compulsory daydream whose images were experts on what he did not want to feel and would rather not imagine. He had just seen an old circus tiger escape from its cage in a cold country and amble bemusedly through a crowd of screaming, fleeing citizens. He had felt the power of its alien gait and then, when it was standing on the edge of a sparse recreational wood where it had gone to look for food, he had seen a bullet crash into its skull in a scatter of blood and bone.

How could he wake from a waking dream? It enveloped everything he thought and everything he looked at. The broken layer of brown and purple cloud scattered in the yellowing sky reminded him of his mother's tortoiseshell comb when he used to close one eye and hold it up to the lamplight and stare at it for ages, until its mottled pattern of light and dark patches filled the whole visual field. That was when he was very little, before he started asking her difficult questions and questioning her easy answers, before they became opponents. Now everyone was his opponent, because he was not in his right mind.

The hills, drenched by the storm, were gleaming and dripping in the afternoon light. How tactless of him to have insisted on bringing his lumbering body to this lovely, liquid scene, to dump it like a sack of cement, split open and hardened by rain, on this otherwise uncontaminated hillside.

On the other hand, he felt such a sense of lightness and of hunger, such a threadbare connection to the rest of human life, that he could easily imagine slipping out of existence, as quietly as one of those bright drops of arrested rain that were falling from the bushes to the grass, and from the grass to the ground.

How could he pit himself against his daughters when they had his whole organization at their command and he had no command of his own disorganization? Organization, disorganization: all these maddening words that treated him as their ventriloquist's dummy, not to mention the images of humanely slaughtered tigers that flickered across the deep gray screen of his television mind, because some bastard, some sadistic sky-god who owned all the channels to all the minds of all living creatures everywhere was playing with the programing and the remote control.

Why go on? Why drag his suffering body into the

next valley? Why endure the anguish of being alive? Because endurance was what he did, thought Dunbar. He hauled himself up and straightened his body one more time and brought both his fists against his chest, inviting that child-devouring sky-god to do his worst, to rain down information from his satellites, to stream his audiovisual hell of white noise and burning bodies straight into Dunbar's fragile brain, to try to split its hemispheres, if he could, to try to strangle him with a word-noose, if he dared.

"Come on," whispered Dunbar hoarsely. "Come on, you bastard."

The next thing that happened was that he forgot the last thing that happened. He let his hands fall to his side, completely absorbed in watching a raindrop change color as it swelled on the tip of a leaf and flashed into the ground. He longed for its fleeting iridescence; he longed to be absorbed into the earth, or, if the earth wouldn't have him, to evaporate into the sky, to become part of everything, with no part in anything: no role, no point, no location, no pattern, and no mind.

Nothing could be done to improve this place, except to remove him from it. He imagined being deleted, like obscene graffiti a teacher wipes off the blackboard before writing out the triumphant formula for a perfectly empty valley. Yes, yes, he must go. Although his knees were begging him to sit down and his lower back was begging him to lie down, and his muscles were begging to have him put down, he started to shuffle meekly through the wet grass, doing his best to get a move on, to respect the valley's very understandable desire to get rid of him. He was a bad man polluting an enchanted space, and the least he could do was to absent himself.

When he had been running a global empire, his cruelty and his vindictiveness and his lies and his tantrums were disguised as the necessary actions of a decisive commander-in-chief, but in his current naked condition the naked character of those actions screamed at him, like ex-prisoners recognizing their torturer in the street, "It's him! It's him! He tore out my fingernails, he splintered my kneecaps, he dissolved my marriage, he forced me to resign, he had me sent to prison . . ." He was too weak to cut their throats and too injured to run away. He was in the unaccustomed position of having to stand there and listen to their point of view. He couldn't sack them or destroy them, they were not his employees or his opponents: they were his memories, recast in the strange light of destitution and vulnerability. It was no use trying to get an injunction against them, or telling his editors to send in the attack dogs to tear apart their reputations; he couldn't even nominate them for ridicule when they were already so busy ridiculing him. All the people he had ever hurt—a veritable crowd, it turned out—were turning their wounds into weapons. He tried to quicken his pace, stumbling once or twice in the effort to escape the enemy memory that was chasing him from, well, from the center of his psyche. He might not be able to outrun what was erupting inside him, but perhaps at the top of this next hill there would be a precipice—if there was any justice or mercy in the world there would be a precipice at the top of the next hill—from which to throw himself head first onto some rocks, to dash his brains out, get his brains right out, perform the necessary surgery, get the trouble out of his head, in an unsparing acknowledgment that the only way to save his life was to end it.

All the things he had ever felt ashamed of seemed to have been distilled into the elixir of his own cruelty. An eye for an eye: that was the law. They were holding him down to clamp his head in a vice and slice his eyelids off. No, please, not that. As he climbed higher his vision grew more blurred, feeding his fear of being blinded by the venom of his accumulated crimes. He clutched his head between his powerful hands, to show how tightly trapped it was, but also in the hope of somehow finding the strength to wrench it aside, to avoid letting the corrosive liquid fall, drop by blistering drop, onto his precious, defenseless eyes. No, please, please, please. His heart was bursting with anguish. He scrambled up the last few yards on all fours and collapsed on the brow of the hill.

For a moment his horror was eclipsed by a further insult to his despair. The slope on the far side was no steeper than the one he had just climbed, all very well for a person who wanted to twist an ankle or break a leg, but by no means adequate for the task he had in mind. Without the comfort of a cliff, there was nothing to do but suffer tamely; he didn't even have the power to organize a swift and particular death.

He would have to linger on, cattle-prodded through a labyrinthine slaughterhouse of hunger, exposure, infection, and insanity, or, worse, be rescued, so that he could be paraded at his daughters' triumph, like a conquered king in chains, pelted with filth and rotten food by the jeering populace.

It was true that in his time he had sacked both Megan and Abigail from key positions in the Dunbar Trust, but only to give them other positions later on and only, always, for their own good, in order to toughen them up and show that unless they could match the suavity and the savagery of his top executives, nepotism would not be allowed to prevail; at any rate, not until the end, when his need for a legacy would make—had made—dynastic considerations paramount. He could now see that if they had misunderstood his motives, the sackings might have set them on the path of revenge. Or perhaps they were angry to be deprived of their mother when they were still so young, perhaps they didn't understand that he was trying to protect them from a mother who was as mad as a snake. He could feel their pain now; feel that if his daughters were monsters it was because he had made them that way. He had tried to make amends, he had given them everything, everything, but when they got it, all they could think of doing was to treat him as he had treated them. And yet he certainly never treated either of them as harshly as he treated Florence. If there was any reason to stay alive it was to sink to his knees to beg Florence's forgiveness, but if there was any reason more pressing than the rest to throw himself off the non-existent cliff he had fondly imagined waiting for him at the top of the hill, it was to express the violence of his sorrow at having maltreated the person he loved most in the world, Catherine's daughter, the only one of his children who had refused to conspire against him, although she had most reason to.

He reached up to protect his eyes, but found that far from being hollowed out by liquid fire, they were wet with ordinary tears. He was surprised, a little indignant, but far too suspicious to be taken in. The fire had been temporarily put out so that his torture could be prolonged, like a hanged man who is cut down so that he can be killed more meticulously. He knew how the world worked: the fireman was an arsonist, the assassin came dressed as a physician, the devil was a bishop harvesting souls for his master, teachers entrusted with children filmed them in the shower and posted their naked bodies on the dark net; he had read the stories, he had read them every morning with his breakfast. Like a puppetmaster who pulls the strings but still has to do the voices for his puppets, Dunbar was partially, if superciliously, merged with his ideal reader: the person who hates chavs and welfare scroungers and perverts and junkies, but also hates toffs and fat cats and tax dodgers and celebrities, in fact the person who hates everybody, except the other people like him, who hate the things that make him feel fear or envy. Dunbar was the man who placed the wafer on their outstretched tongues, transubstantiating the corrosive passivity of fear and envy into the dynamic single-mindedness of hatred. As the high priest of this low practice, he had to admit that in his astonishing new circumstances the view from the altar rail was barely distinguishable from blindness.

If he was not allowed to kill himself straight away, it was because he didn't deserve to get away so lightly; if his eyes had been temporarily spared, it was so that images of a more intimate horror could imprint themselves on his fading vision and haunt his forthcoming blindness. He searched about for some way to evade his fate. He thought he could make out a talus in the distance, surmounted by a tiny cliff. In his current condition he would need a helicopter to get there, but the last thing he wanted was an amiable and trustworthy pilot encouraging him to admire the view and not to go too near the edge.

He sat up on his knees and clambered painfully to his feet in order to take in a wider view of his surroundings. Neither the valley behind him nor the one ahead contained buildings or structures of any sort: no gates or stiles or walls. Even the Herdwick sheep that had accompanied him on most of his journey so far seemed to find these denuded hills and snowy peaks too remote to venture into. The phrase "in the middle of nowhere" came to Dunbar with the original force that underlies the destructive popularity of cliché. Yes, he was in the middle of nowhere—that was exactly the right phrase. He had always lived and worked in central locations of one sort or another and there was a certain sense of continuity in discovering that he had pulled it off again, even if the place he was in the middle of this time was nowhere, even if the satisfaction of finding an address could not entirely make up for the absence of any shelter, any protection from the icy air trickling through the cracks in his clothing, of any food, or any fire. He was starting to shiver and to feel that marrow numbness that made him dread the onset of night.

"Help!"

Dunbar knew that he was alone and was at a loss to explain the voice he had just heard.

"What?" he called out.

"Help!"

He thought for a moment that it might be the helicopter pilot, the last person to have taken shape in his mind, but he saw no evidence of his existence—if he was a helicopter pilot, where was his helicopter? It just didn't add up.

His bewilderment turned to alarm as he watched what seemed to be a low mound crack open and take on a human shape. A man in a filthy brown overcoat, his beard loaded with earth, sat up, brushed some of the dirt from his face, and reiterated his request.

"Help," he said, "help me get these boots off. They're killing me."

"Just like my daughters," said Dunbar, amazed by the coincidence. With a rush of solidarity, he knelt down beside his groaning new acquaintance and started to unlace his mud-caked boots.

"I can hardly feel my feet anymore and when I do, I wish I didn't. Nothing but blisters."

"I have blisters on my eyes," said Dunbar.

"Can you see anything?"

"Hardly a thing," said Dunbar.

"'If the blind lead the blind, both shall fall into the ditch,' Matthew 15:14."

"Sounds like a sensible fellow," said Dunbar. "You're much better off with a guide dog."

"I was a vicar—the Reverend Simon Field—but I lost my way: I fell into that ditch of which Matthew speaks."

"You look more like a tramp than a vicar," said Dunbar bluntly.

"I am a hermit."

"That's what you call a vicar who turns into a tramp," said Dunbar. "Well, I'm a bum, that's what you call a billionaire who turns into a tramp."

"My gambling got the better of me," said Simon. "I let them strip the lead from the church roof to pay off my debts."

"Jesus," said Dunbar, "look at the state of your feet, they're bleeding."

"The copper piping went next," said Simon. "I lost a bet on the outcome of the general election. I thought compassion would prevail, but we live in the age of aspiration, the amphetamine of the masses. After they carried the big old radiators out of the church, I had to announce to the parish that we'd been robbed."

Dunbar tucked what remained of Simon's socks into the neck of his boots, lowered his cupped hands into a clear puddle of fresh rainwater and poured the cool liquid over Simon's traumatized feet.

"My mistake was to confess to the chair of the

Church Roof Committee. I thought we were in love, but he sold my story to the press."

"*Gay Vicar Puts Lead in His Pencil*," said Dunbar, drying Simon's feet with his scarf.

"Oh, I see you're familiar with the campaign," said Simon. "'*Gay Vicar loses his frock . . . as bent as the lead he sold to cover his gambling debts . . .*' and so on and so forth."

"I know, I know," said Dunbar, "we shouldn't have hounded you that way. I'm glad the rumors about your suicide are untrue. My editor wrote to me saying, 'I see that pouf priest topped himself. Good riddance.' I told him that was going too far, I told him that was in very poor taste—we didn't publish that, obviously."

"I don't care about all that now," said Simon. "I know of a cave nearby where we could rest for the night. It'll give us some protection from the cold. I'll show you the way, if you like."

"Thank you," said Dunbar, helping to put Simon's boots back on. "That's very kind of you, especially considering—"

"Never mind all that," said Simon. "Let's just make our way to the cave. Now that it's stopped raining we might be able to get a fire going."

Dunbar gave Simon a hand and hoisted him to his feet. A gaudy sunset, like a drunken farewell scrawled in lipstick on a mirror, formed the background to their departure, but soon the color drained from the sky, leaving a glassy gray clarity in the air. Simon hobbled forward and with each halting step he looked as if he was about to go down on one knee but just managed to rise again at the last moment. Dunbar, who was in awe of his new companion, started to imitate his walk, and with each partial genuflexion, silhouetted against the ghostly light cast by the snow on the distant peaks, he imagined that he was going down on his knees to beg the forgiveness, one after another, of all the people he had harmed.

12

At three in the morning, despite popping a couple of Klonopin, Dr. Bob was lying in bed staring at the ceiling like a man who had just been given an electric shock. He listened with disgust to an owl hooting in a nearby tree. To his movie-going, metropolitan ear it felt like the soundtrack that an idiotic, not to say malicious editor had failed to cut out of the harrowing scene in which the protagonist lies on his bed, *understandably worried*. It had been a hectic day, what with the immolation of Peter Walker (a reckless extravagance), and the fruitless rush to Nutting and to all the other places that Dunbar might conceivably have reached since his escape. He seemed to have spent the whole afternoon turning around in muddy yards after watching Kevin, through the rain-splattered windows of the Range Rover, interrogating concerned but clueless Cumbrians, their blue overalls, big sweaters, and bedraggled livestock forming the blurred background to the sharply delineated words "No Service" in the

corner of his phone. Finding Dunbar was now inci-
dental to his purposes; the arrival of Cogniccenti's
money was not.

When he finally managed to get back to the King's
Head and was able to get on the internet, he discovered that his bank balance was unaltered since the six
and a half million paid into it by the Dunbar Trust the
week before. His Geneva bank was already closed, but
his personal account manager, who had been primed
for the arrival of twenty-five million dollars, had written an email offering to chase up the money, if Dr. Bob
would kindly furnish him with a reference for its
source. Given the service that Swiss banks were supposed to provide, he felt there was something highly
unethical about being asked to divulge the origins of
any assets whatsoever. He wrote back an austere email
saying that he simply wished to be advised as soon as
the funds arrived and that he would chase them up
from "his end." There had been no time, however, to
call Cogniccenti before dinner and it would have been
inept to leave the trace of an importunate email, although he was longing to dash off a dollar sign with
twenty-five question marks after it.

The weather cleared up in the late afternoon and
the forecast was good for Tuesday, allowing Abigail to
contact Jim Sage during dinner and tell him to pick
up Kevin and J by helicopter in the morning from the
Plumdale sports field, the only piece of flat ground
they had been able to identify. Dr. Bob would be staying behind with Abby and Meg, ready to respond by
car as soon as the helicopter team had located Dun-

bar. They would have plenty to do in the hotel, dealing with the questions that arose from the imminent Board meeting, and keeping the lines of credit in place for their buyout. In the meantime, a great deal of ingenuity had to go into hiding the latest trading figures out of China. If the market picked up any scent of those successes, the Dunbar share price would skyrocket before the sisters could buy them back, or indeed be outbid by an opponent in possession of the full facts. The pleasure of working so cunningly on Cogniccenti's behalf was blunted by the absence of his twenty-five-million-dollar traitor's fee.

He would have to wait until he was sure that Abby and Meg were fully asleep before calling Cogniccenti. Fortunately, Abby had been too tired to summon him to her bed, while Meg was suffering from an undisguised hunger for Jesus's muscle-bound caresses, and judging by the thudding of the bedhead on the party wall, as well as her rather ostentatious cries of startled pleasure, she was still fully aroused. Dr. Bob was of course relieved that Meg did not require his attention, and was naturally contemptuous of his noisy, knuckleheaded replacement, but he was rather surprised to find how jealous he felt as well. Both sisters belonged to him. He couldn't stand either of them, indeed he was about to betray both of them, but that was no reason for them to stop desiring him or stop depending on him. There was no satisfaction in betraying people who had already defected. Like the demented sheepdog in *Far from the Madding Crowd*, he was planning to drive his little flock over the edge of a cliff, but however twisted his purpose he still took pride in his basic skill and could not complacently allow one of his victims to wander off on her own.

What was he doing comparing himself to a sheepdog in a movie? It was true that they had seen a couple of sheepdogs during the day. Perhaps the Klonopin was loosening his thinking into a more associative, hypnagogic drift, but even the thought that this might be the case gave him a fresh shock of anxiety. How could he have been so naive? Cogniccenti needed nothing more from him: he knew the timing of the deal and was pre-empting it; Dr. Bob had provided one valuable detail after another: the banks the sisters were using, the Board members that were most risk averse, the size and terms of the debt that Eagle Rock would be incurring in its buyout. With an unprecedented lack of paranoia, he had given Cogniccenti everything, and the worst of it was that his enemy, as he had now started to think of him, knew that he was in no position to go back to the sisters. What would he say? "I was going to betray you, but now it looks like the guy I was going to betray you to is going to betray me, so I want to betray him." It was not a confidence-inspiring pitch.

That fucking owl, hooting again! The sheepdog was herding the falling sheep, falling asleep. The owl and the sheepdog jumped over the moon, or went to sea in a sieve, or the owl and the sheepdog fell over a cliff; they were all sheep falling over a cliff into sleep, falling into sleep through a steep gray space with no ground.

It was still dark when Dunbar woke up, but there was enough moonlight for him to see the steam from his breath melting in the bitter air. He realized that, just like Simon, he could no longer feel his feet. That was obviously what happened to people who lived out here. The hollow under a ledge of jutting rock was not quite the cave that Simon had promised, but it was a form of shelter, sloping downward and therefore drier than the surrounding ground.

There had once been a man called Henry Dunbar, an expert on the glories and shortcomings of some of the greatest properties in the world, but he was barely discernible now, familiar yet lost, like the pattern in a blind bleached by the sun; it was the man freezing to death under a ledge of rock who was the real Dunbar, with the numbness spreading from his hands and feet toward his heart, a heart that had never pumped so hard, or felt so much, but that would soon come to a stop on this frigid mountainside.

"Simon!" he called out. "Simon!"

There was no reply. Dunbar sat up, too cold to shiver. He fumbled for the torch in the inside pocket of his overcoat and managed to shine it around the little hollow. There was no one to be seen. Where had Simon gone? He was a religious man; he wouldn't just abandon Dunbar. He must have gone to fetch help, or fetch some food he had hidden nearby. He had better come back soon, or Dunbar would die alone in this horrible darkness, alone and unforgiven.

————

Florence woke up with her heart pounding. Her father was in serious trouble; she could feel the life leaking out of him into the thirsty ground. She had dreamt that he was under a ledge of rock, freezing to death. She started to get dressed although it wouldn't begin to be light for another hour and a half. The police and the mountain rescue were going to begin at dawn. They were bringing a helicopter and she was following in one of her own.

Mark didn't blame Florence for her distrust, although he was a little hurt that she went to no trouble to disguise it. He could not convince anyone that he was siding against his wife rather than spying on her behalf, since honesty and deceit, in the absence of some crucial information or irreversible risk, would both take the same form: a fervent profession of sincerity. He longed to offer a concrete sacrifice or a crucial gift, but his cold war with Abby had long excluded him from her plans and projects. The two of them occasionally converged, barely exchanging a word in the back of the limo that delivered them to the fundraising dinner or the award ceremony and barely exchanging impressions when it returned them to their vast apartment. The apartment itself was conveniently spread over three floors, with Mark's set of rooms sharing the lowest floor with the kitchen and the pool, the gym and the guest bedrooms, and the screening room, while Abby occupied the penthouse. In between were the great entertainment spaces in which Mark was seldom seen. When they converged for Christmas, or Easter, or for a week at Home Lake in the summer, they showed the same practiced ennui as the representatives of enemy countries listening to translations of each other's speeches in the United Nations General Assembly Hall.

With so much distance between them it was hard to get excited about a separation. Mark was from a family whose money was so old that by the time he met Abby most of it had disintegrated and turned to dust. His pedigree suited her and her immense fortune suited him. One of Mark's ancestors (the first Mark Rush) had been a Puritan dissenter who crossed the Atlantic on the *Mayflower*. How could he have known, as he lurched from side to side on that creaking deck, in his dreary black clothes, muttering prayers and scolding his family, that he was on board one of the most fashionable ships in all of history, one that would leave Cleopatra's barge languishing in the perfumed air as an exotic irrelevance? The great-grandson of that *Mayflower* passenger decided to try his hand at farming on Manhattan. The farm was only a marginal success until his grandson started harvesting streets and squares from the fields and orchards whose traditional crops had yielded such a mediocre income. The family's fortune peaked in the late nineteenth century, but was large enough to

withstand several generations of elegant mismanage-
ment and, when they became all the rage, expensive
divorces.

By the time the twenty-three-year-old Abby Dunbar met the latest Mark Rush, he turned out to be a
weak but emphatically handsome, immensely well-
connected, and officially well-educated bachelor, with
a big family house up the Hudson that he hadn't
been forced to sell yet. It was a combination of qualities that seemed to suit Abby perfectly, and she soon
decided that she would much rather be a Rush than
some French or Italian countess, or the recently married heiress who was supposed to renew the three-
acre roof of an inherited headache in England.

Despite its enthusiastic beginning, Mark's marriage very soon lost all its vitality and finally expired
with the discovery that Abby was unable to have children. After that, without either of them being in the
least permissive by nature, they granted each other
the freedom to do what the hell they liked. Indifference and opportunity did the work that tolerance
might have done in other circumstances. Mark would
often fly down to South Carolina to shoot quail with
old friends, taking Mindy, his long-standing mistress,
whose old family fortune had shaded even more emphatically than Mark's into new family poverty, but
whose company was reminiscent of the uncompli-
cated days when his parents' friends dropped their
children round to the house to play with him in the
garden or the nursery. She felt like the most natural
companion in the world.

Although Mark would have been prepared to maintain this state of affairs indefinitely, Abby had managed to disrupt his complacency by kidnapping her father and locking him up in a sanatorium. It just wasn't right. When Mark's own grandfather, a foul-tempered tyrant, had become increasingly eccentric and fundamentally forgetful, the family had kept him in the old place upstate, because it was the right thing to do. What you did in a situation like that was to create a marvelous fund of grandfather anecdotes—the time he fell asleep at the wheel and drifted into a neighbor's field, killing his prize racehorse; the time he insisted on climbing onto the roof, wearing his quilted silk dressing gown from Turnbull & Asser in London, to clean out the gutters with Harold, the old caretaker; the time he shot at the postman, mistaking him for a Japanese soldier; priceless stories that more than made up for the strains of taking the high road.

When something wasn't right, it wasn't right. An impulse, partly moral, partly ancestral, and partly caused by the discharge of a long-withheld hatred for his wife, had made him step up to the plate and try to help rescue that old patriarch, his father-in-law, to whom, in the end, they all owed their supremely comfortable lives. If only he could be more useful, thought Mark regretfully, picking up the phone to place his breakfast order. He wanted to share his troubles with Mindy; she often had terrific ideas and practical advice, but it was too early to call her yet, so he might as well have some poached eggs and kippers sent up to the room. He hadn't had kippers for ages.

The sunlight crept into the hollow where Dunbar's almost frozen body lay curled up in his immense overcoat. The faint heat from the rays landing on the uncovered parts of his face and the pink light irradiating his eyelids made him realize that he was alive.

He could not have given any account of his mental life over the last few hours, although he was convinced it had not consisted of sleep, just blankness without rest.

He opened his eyelids tentatively; they fluttered for a while until he was able to squint steadily at the opening of his shallow cave. There seemed to be someone kneeling there.

"Simon?"

"Yes."

"Where have you been?" asked Dunbar in an urgent, reproachful whisper. "I almost died last night. I doubt I've got the strength to move."

"Come on," said Simon, "it's time to leave. I've come to take you to a better place. This was just a little shelter for the night. We have hot food waiting for us in a farmhouse nearby. I've been sent to collect you. It's less than a mile."

"I can't move. To be honest, I wish I had slipped away during the night."

"You can slip away another time; right now you should have some breakfast. 'To every thing there is a season, and a time to every purpose under the heaven: A time to be born, and a time to die; a time to plant,

and a time to pluck up that which is planted.' Eccle-
siastes 3:1."

"Yes, yes," said Dunbar impatiently; "they always
read that at funerals. Now give me a hand, will you?"

Simon helped him to his feet. Dunbar staggered
about for a while, trying to get his balance.

"I can hardly stand," he protested. "Ah, my feet, my
feet are stinging me. It's as if my boots were full of
scorpions. Ah, damn and blast, my feet!"

"That's a good sign: the blood is coming back, you
won't be losing any of your toes. Come on, it's this
way," said Simon, setting off slowly. "There's a farmhouse just around the corner at the bottom of the hill."

"And they're expecting us?" asked Dunbar.

"Oh, yes, everything is being made ready."

Dunbar rested a hand on Simon's shoulder and
started to hobble forward. He found that it took all
his concentration to walk and he was unable to go on
talking at the same time. Simon tactfully fell in with
Dunbar's state of mind and the two men carried on
in silence.

J was a total fucking cunt, in Kevin's opinion, and a
duffer, a complete fucking duffer, shagging that bitch
all night and turning up at breakfast like a zombie,
a zombie with a fucking grin on his face. They had
all done it, obviously. Kevin had banged her brains
out, nympho bitch, got her screaming, but not on the
night before a big op. Now he had to give J a couple of
Modafinil to keep his eyelids unstuck, stupid fucking

cunt. Dr. Bob made your nasty neighborhood dealer look like the vicar at a treatment center: he'd give you anything you asked for, plus a lot of things you hadn't even heard of, but he wouldn't be resupplying them until they got back to the States, and the truth was that Kevin had been chucking back the Modafinil like a kid with a tube of Smarties. He liked to be wired, liked to be sharp, hated coming down, and he was pissed off with J for bleeding his supply—fucking cunt.

"Yo, Kevin," said J coming back into the lobby with his rucksack on his back, dressed for action, "I'm feeling a whole lot better. Fact is, I feel great."

"You don't say?" said Kevin, approaching J and lowering his voice. "Could that be because you nicked my last two fucking speed pills?"

Kevin had eight left, which would just be enough to get him back to New York.

"I thought they were for both of us."

"They're for me to distribute as and when I see fit," said Kevin.

"Like to yourself, the whole time," said J, light-heartedly.

"Don't you fucking question my orders," hissed Kevin, coming in close to J's ear. "You may have just shagged the boss, but in this little army I'm your commanding officer."

"Yes, sir," said J.

Kevin was too wired to know whether J's obedience was sarcastic or not, but in either case the lobby of the King's Head was not the place to take him apart.

The two men walked out of the hotel and crossed the road to the playing fields. Jim Sage was there with a helicopter, talking to a woman in an overcoat and scarf.

"Hi, there, boys," said Jim, opening the door of the helicopter, "welcome aboard. I was just explaining to this lady that I had to make an emergency landing so that we could effect a rescue."

Kevin piled into the helicopter without a word.

"Yo, Jim, my man!" said J, giving the avuncular pilot a virile hug. "That's right, ma'am," he said, turning to the local resident, "we've got a life to save."

His eyes misted over for a moment and then he punched himself in the chest surprisingly hard.

"Feel the love," he gasped.

"Get in the fucking chopper before I throw up," said Kevin.

Poor Henry, thought Wilson, no one was more ill suited to a crash course in self-knowledge, especially one that was being imposed on him so late in life. What was it that Richard the Second said, "I was not born to sue, but to command"? That was old Dunbar in one line, except that he preferred "Just make it happen," the command without the commentary. In fact, you might say that Richard's line should have been, "I was not born to command but to comment." Dissipating his initiatives in perfect descriptions of his woeful states had never been Henry's problem. In fact, he had always lived in the future; rushing ahead so fast he didn't have time to even sketch what was happening along the way, let alone beguile it with rhetoric. The goals were always clear, but the experience around them hazy. Wherever Henry was, Wilson just hoped he had a map. If he had a map, he would have a target, and if he had a target he'd make it.

Hearing someone knock, Wilson got up to open his door. He vaguely expected to see Florence or Chris, but soon resigned himself to welcoming Mark into his room instead.

"Oh, wow, this is a great view of Buttermere," said Mark, moving over to the bay window in Wilson's room. "I guess we have Abby to thank for introducing us to another charming hotel," he added with a facetious chuckle.

"What's on your mind?" asked Wilson.

"I've been talking to my friend Mindy," Mark began.

"I know Mindy," said Wilson, irritated by the epithet "friend" for a woman Mark had been in a parallel marriage with for ten years.

"Well, she just reminded me of something I told her a couple of weeks ago. You know better than anyone how one gets used to seeing and hearing some pretty big sums in this family, so I forgot about it just as soon as I told her."

"Yes?"

"I happened to be in Abby's study, I wasn't snooping; I was looking for a print cartridge. Anyhow, I saw a little notepad on her desk and one of the things on it was '6.5' and an arrow and then B. Now, I just have a hunch, and it's only a hunch, that she was making a big payment to Dr. Bob."

"She was," said Wilson; "we know about that. It was all done in the open. He's going to join the Board and on top of the usual payment to Board members he was given a bonus for 'years of devoted service' as Dunbar's personal physician."

"Oh," said Mark, "you knew about that."

"I'm on very good terms with most of the Board and they're keeping me in the loop. What would be really useful is any evidence of malpractice on Dr. Bob's part, proof that the devoted service has been to Abby and Meg, not to Henry."

"Well, how on earth am I supposed to get that?" asked Mark.

"Why don't you ask your friend Mindy," said Wilson, leading the crestfallen Mark back to the door. "I've got to talk to Florence before she takes off. We've got a helicopter coming to help look for Henry."

"Can I go along?" asked Mark.

"It's only got three seats. We're just following the police in case they find him. Florence and Chris are on board and we just can't afford to ditch the pilot," said Wilson, "even for you."

With any luck, thought Abby, as she watched Jim's helicopter disappear down the valley toward Nutting, they would find her father dead. That would be the simplest solution. Chasing after him was taking up a lot of time and they really ought to be back in New York by now, preparing for the most important moment in the company's history: taking the Dunbar Trust private again, in a move that would put one of the most powerful media organizations on the planet entirely under their control. It was time for old Dunbar to move on, to stop clinging to power and stop obstructing what he really ought to be proud of, his two oldest daughters taking the company back in hand. They had it all planned: thirty percent of the employees would be invited to reimagine their futures, sentimental titles would be sold off, and the whole company would become a minting machine, granting them the universal access that their father had earned but jealously guarded for himself. They would seek the approval of the Board on Thursday and, after signing a few legal forms, the directors would be free to leave the building in the knowledge that they would be considerably richer when the deal closed and that they would be in serious trouble if they breathed a word to anyone of what was going on.

Abby heard her telephone purring from the table behind her. She glanced at it and saw that the call was from Dr. Harris. He was the last person she wanted to speak to, but the authorities might have contacted him with some important information—preferably the discovery of her father's dead body.

"Yes, Dr. Harris, what can I do for you?"

"Well, Mrs. Rush, the best thing you can do for

yourself would be to call the police and offer to cooperate fully."

"Cooperate with what?" asked Abby. "The inquiry into your incompetence?"

"The inquiry into the part you have played in the events leading to Peter Walker's suicide."

"Suicide?"

"Yes, I'm sorry to say that, despite all our precautions, Peter hanged himself in the shower early this morning. It's an appalling and quite unnecessary death for which I am determined to hold you to account."

"You're holding *me* responsible," said Abby, instantly furious, "for letting a tormented alcoholic escape from your sanatorium, dragging my old and, let's face it, extremely important father with him and endangering both their lives! Let's hope my father isn't found dead as well, or you'll be on trial for *two* counts of manslaughter. Please don't hesitate to put your accusations in writing, Dr. Harris, so I can sue you for defamation of character."

"Oh, I have put them in writing, Mrs. Rush, and so has Nurse Roberts—"

"That idiot! I can't wait to see a pack of QCs unkenneled on her—"

"Peter told us what you did to him, Mrs. Rush," Dr. Harris interrupted her quietly but firmly, "and we have no doubt that he was telling the truth. He was an alcoholic, but he was a highly intelligent man and in no way psychotic."

"Oh, for God's sake, he was a famous mess," said Abby, "who couldn't speak in his own voice—except to whimper."

"Well, I'm sure you know all about that," said Dr. Harris.

Abby immediately ended the call and dropped her phone on the table.

"Fuck!" she shouted at the top of her voice. "Fuck! Fuck! Fuck!"

Why was this happening? What had she done to deserve a complication like this when she was on the verge of a great victory? It was *so* unfair!

Dunbar lost his balance on some loose stones and almost toppled over.

"Mind where you're going," he grumbled to Simon; "it's too steep along here. I can hardly walk on level ground, let alone down this sort of landslide you've got us on."

Ever since that stupid, stupid accident a year ago in Davos, what he dreaded most, or at least one of the things he most dreaded, was falling over. It was a bad idea in the first place to gather all the most important people in the world and pack them into the icy streets of a skiing resort in January, for a summit, or a "Forum" as they liked to call it—exactly the wrong word, really, since no one ever needed a special invitation or one of those fought-over white badges to go to a public square or a marketplace. He had arrived in Davos that afternoon two hours later than scheduled and was hurrying to a crucial meeting, an off-Forum, behind-the-scenes meeting, the only sort that mattered. The snow was pelting down softly, which normally would have helped, but some Forum zealot had scraped away all the fresh powder, leaving a patch of black ice on the path to Zhou's chalet. Dunbar was powering up to the front door when he flipped over and fell on his back, hitting his head on the ground. He had been made to look ridiculous; he had lost face in front of a bloody Politburo face merchant. His obsession with punctuality had cost him six weeks in hospital, and he hadn't got the satellite broadcasting deal he had spent a year setting up. Things had never been quite the same since that time. That's when his real fall started: the slow-motion fall that he'd been in over the last year, the one he was still trying to avoid bringing to a fatal conclusion on this slippery wreck of a hillside.

"You don't seem to have much to say for yourself today," said Dunbar, tightening his grip on Simon's shoulder. "I don't know how you cope with all this walking."

If the clutching muscles and weeping tendons in his legs got any worse, he would have to stop moving altogether. He was now fully committed to Simon's peculiar buckling gait, the concession made to knees that could not stand the next obligatory step. If only his exhaustion could overwhelm his fear, he would willingly lie down and die, but for the moment his fear was overwhelming his exhaustion and he must keep moving.

In his eyes, the landscape had now taken on the sort of pliancy and suggestiveness usually reserved for passing clouds. Its wild plasticity was checked by the narrow choice of forms that it conjured up. Dunbar saw only a series of crouching animals, often piebald with snow, their heads rearing up, their mouths jutting forward, their limbs extended in spurs, or planted underground to give their assault a more deadly impetus. Over to his left was one of Cerberus's monstrous heads, which might be woken by the clatter of a loose stone, or the thud of a falling body. The rounded back of his serpent's tail, pretending to be a hill, disappeared a few hundred yards away but might surface at any moment under Dunbar's bruised feet. The spurs jutting out from the mountain to his right were the outstretched limbs of a Sphinx, its claws embedded in the earth. He didn't dare look behind him at the open jaws of the white-backed wolf waiting for a final surge in the fluidity of the rock to leap forward and tear out his throat. He really must get to Simon's farmhouse hidden round the bend of this crumbling hill, round the bend in this devouring landscape. He hoped that Simon knew what he was doing and wasn't misleading him in some way. He seemed oddly silent today. Mind you, people often fell silent around him, even presidents and prime ministers. They were waiting, hoping for his benediction: "I had my doubts about your government, Maggie, until you started shooting terrorists in the back . . . I understand your strategy, Mr. President, and you can count on our support . . . I'm afraid all you've achieved, Bernanke, is to turn a private debt crisis into a public debt crisis."

"Hang on!" said Dunbar, suddenly thrown out of his reverie and flushed with panic, "can you hear that thudding in the air? Quickly! Run!"

He let go of Simon's shoulder and started to totter forward as fast as his excruciated legs would allow him, heading toward the nearest boulder that he might be able to hide behind. Helicopter gunships were on their way, their side doors open, their mounted machine guns ready. To them he would look like just another Vietcong sympathizer or Taliban insurgent whose back should be streaked with gunfire, sliced open from kidney to shoulder. A strange energy took over Dunbar's decrepit body, a kind of ecstatic terror that made him feel that he was vaulting over the sometimes stony and sometimes sodden ground. The sound was growing stronger and he wasn't sure where the helicopters were by the time he reached the boulder. As the roaring machine swept overhead, he crouched down with his back against the rock and his head between his knees, praying that he had not been seen.

Although he had managed to fall asleep toward dawn, Dr. Bob had almost immediately been woken by rage and anxiety at the thought of his imperiled pension scheme. With three nights of acute insomnia in succession, his thinking was full of sheer falls, downward spirals, and flitting ghosts. He had already betrayed Dunbar, and then betrayed the daughters with whom he had betrayed Dunbar, but now he had been out-betrayed by Cogniccenti. His financial security was under threat, his Machiavellian pride wounded, and his mind caught between the contradictory but equally turbulent currents of tiredness and aggression. The only thing he knew with any certainty was that he must do something twisted, more twisted than his thoroughly twisted opponents, but the details proved surprisingly hard to work out.

He had already concluded that it was too dangerous to betray Cogniccenti through Abby and Meg, since it would be impossible to disguise the fact that he had intended to betray them. Improvising a little wildly, he thought he might help Florence to find her father first and then get an anonymous message to her that the Dunbar Trust was under threat from Unicom. The old man could rally the troops, somehow. In any case, the Board would screw up Cogniccenti's plans, and undermine Abby and Meg, for whom he now had such a resolute loathing that, whatever happened, he was determined that they should fail.

Looking out of the window of the King's Head dining room, Dr. Bob spotted George, the faithful retainer who annoyed Abby with his solicitous and respectful questions about her father. He had been Dunbar's driver, whenever he was in Europe, for over thirty years and could easily be persuaded to do any-thing that was presented as being in the old man's best interests.

"Can you hear me?" said Chris through the microphone on his headset.

Florence smiled and nodded.

"Okay, so the pilot is talking on a different circuit
and we can have a private conversation. If he needs to
talk to us, he'll warn us."

"Great," said Florence, "because I don't want anyone except us to know what I arranged with Jim. It
could get him into trouble."

"Understood," said Chris. "Be discreet with your
phone because the pilot can't technically allow you to
use it, although it doesn't interfere with the navigation."

Florence nodded again and reached out for Chris's
hand.

Their helicopter swayed backward slightly as it
lifted off the hotel lawn and then swooped forward in
a curving path over the lake.

Luckily Kevin and J were too busy bickering to notice
what Jim thought he had seen. He couldn't take the
risk of going back to check before texting the coor-
dinates to Florence. He had agreed to give her a five-
minute start.

"Do you know a place called Adam's Hough?" said
Chris to the pilot.

"He can't hear you," Florence reminded him.

"Right," said Chris, smiling and tapping the pilot on the shoulder.

"I'll contact the police," said Florence.

Chris nodded and made a sign to the pilot to turn on his headphones.

"Come on. Let's go," said Abby, clapping her hands at Dr. Bob as she swept through the dining room. Meg was behind her, wearing dark glasses and yawning. "Jim has texted me saying that Daddy has been spotted."

"At last, some good news," said Dr. Bob, following the sisters to the front of the hotel.

"Take us to Adam's Hough," said Abby to George, as she got into the Range Rover.

"And don't spare the horses," said Dr. Bob to George as he got into the passenger seat next to him.

"Oy, Jimbo," said Kevin, "we're looking for an eighty-year-old businessman, not a marathon runner training for the fucking Olympics. Turn around."

"I guess you're right," said Jim; "he probably didn't make it this far."

"Of course I'm right, fuckwit," said Kevin.

Jim began a very leisurely curve back toward the place he thought he had seen Dunbar five minutes earlier. He had just told Abby, without the foul-mouthed mercenaries noticing, but hoped that Florence would get there first.

Dunbar fumbled in his pocket and got hold of his Swiss Army knife. He eventually managed to pull out the main blade with his gnarled and frozen fingers. He clasped the handle of the knife and stabbed the air a couple of times with the blade. When they tried to take him prisoner, he would take one of them with him; he would go down fighting. He was Henry Dunbar and nobody could mess with Henry Dunbar without paying a price.

He turned around and peeped over the edge of the boulder, wondering where Simon had gone. The hillside and the valley below were completely empty. He knew that there was something funny about his sense of time, but he was genuinely surprised that Simon had been able to disappear in what seemed like only a few minutes. Still, it might be better that way. Simon was a man of the cloth, probably no use in a fight.

"Mano-a-mano," muttered Dunbar, "against my daughters' trained assassins."

He tilted his head. They were on their way. He could hear helicopter blades throbbing through the air.

"You're going in the wrong direction, you moron!" Abby shouted.

"Oh, dear," said George, "are you quite sure? I do apologize."

Abby showed Megan her phone to confirm that the

pulsing blue dot of their current location was moving farther away from their destination.

Megan, who had been rather lethargic until then, suddenly became animated.

"Get out of the car!" she said.

"I do apologize," said George.

"Get out!" she screamed.

"What for?" asked George.

"I'm going to drive, you idiot."

George stopped the car and stepped out apprehensively. Megan pushed past him and got into the driving seat, pulling the door closed.

"I'm going to run the fucker over," said Megan.

"You are not," said Dr. Bob, tugging at the handbrake, "I forbid it."

"You what?" laughed Megan.

"Oh, Meg," said Abby, "he's probably right. I forgot to tell you, Peter whatshisname, that awful comedian, committed suicide. There are going to be legal complications."

"You forgot to tell us?" said Dr. Bob.

"Well, I've had a lot on my mind," said Abby.

"Okay, okay, let's just go," said Megan.

Dr. Bob released the handbrake.

"I told you not to set him on fire," said Dr. Bob.

"Oh, do stop harping on it," said Abby.

Before he had time to reply, Megan had reversed the car swiftly over George's feet, changed gears, and driven forward over them a second time.

"Whoops, sorry!" she cooed, over the sound of George's screams.

"Jesus, Megan!" said Dr. Bob, "let me out of the car."

"Why?"

"To see how much damage you've done. I'm a doctor, in case you've forgotten."

"In case *I've* forgotten?" said Megan. "You didn't take a Hippocratic oath, sweetheart, you took a hypocrite's oath, in case *you've* forgotten."

She sped off down the road.

Dr. Bob looked back at George lying on the roadside, clutching his shins to keep the weight of his crushed feet off the ground. George had served his purpose and with any luck would have delayed them enough to give Florence the advantage. Still, all this violence was so frivolous, so typical of the spoilt brats he had to work with. He was going to have to go back afterward and clear up the damage caused by Megan's childish vindictiveness. He felt a wave of hatred for these two women who were brought up expecting every mess they made to be cleared up after them. Hearing the faint chime of an incoming message, he pulled the phone out of his pocket and glanced down at the screen.

"*I am pleased to report that the funds have successfully arrived, with many apologies for the delay. Kind Regards, Kristoff Richter-Gulag.*"

Shit. Okay. Patience had never been one of his greatest strengths. Still, he hadn't yet done anything fundamentally wrong; given that he was now back in alliance with Cogniccenti. Nothing irrevocable, although Cogniccenti was expecting Dunbar to be taken out of circulation, rather than returned to New York in time for the Board meeting.

If only he could think straight. Perhaps he should warn Dunbar anyway, not tell him the whole thing, but just enough to bring down Meg and Abby. If Cogniccenti won, they would lose power, but the value of their shares would shoot up, making them even more redundantly rich. He wanted to see them destroyed and humiliated. The hatred he felt right now might well be the most authentic emotion he had ever experienced. It had to be included in his pension scheme, not just the money.

Florence made her way through the snow and bracken toward the boulder that she knew her father was hiding behind.

"Henry?" she called. "Daddy? It's Florence."

She saw the top half of Dunbar's head appear over the stone's upper edge.

"It's Florence," she repeated.

Dunbar gradually emerged, his white hair matted and filthy, his face unshaven and emaciated, his overcoat streaked with mud; a penknife thrust forward in his right hand. He looked at Florence with astonishment, not knowing what to make of her appearance.

"I'm here to look after you," said Florence.

Still holding the penknife in his hand, he allowed his arm to drop by his side.

"After all I've done," said Dunbar.

"After all you've been through," she said.

Florence moved closer until she was within reach of her father.

"We must bring Simon with us as well," said Dunbar, tears filling his eyes. "He's been very badly treated and we should do something to help him."

"We will," said Florence. "Where is he?"

"I'm not sure . . . I get confused more easily than before. He was here until a moment ago."

"Come back with us and the police will look for Simon," said Florence.

"We mustn't let him die," said Dunbar, sobbing. "You must find him."

"We will," said Florence. "Don't worry."

"I have been very worried," said Dunbar.

"I know, Daddy," said Florence, "but it's all right now."

Letting the penknife fall, Dunbar stepped forward, resting both his hands on Florence's shoulders.

"We have a stretcher for you," said Florence.

"I think I can walk if you help me," said Dunbar.

Florence put her arm around her father's waist and he put his arm around her shoulder and the two of them picked their way slowly through the patches of snow and the brown winter bracken toward the waiting helicopters.

13

"He's asleep," said Chris, coming out of Dunbar's bedroom into the main cabin of the plane. "The doctor says that he's happy to come down to London with us, but his passport is in Keswick so he can't come on to New York. He thinks Henry is in reasonable shape physically, given what he's been through, but that he's quite delusional."

"Well, surely he needs to get as much sleep as possible," said Florence. "Do we really have to go via London?"

"Believe me, I've weighed it up carefully," said Wilson. "I've persuaded the solicitors to come out to Farnborough airport, so Henry won't even have to move from his bed, but there are certain things we can do legally, if we act quickly, that will potentially give us a significant edge over your sisters. Then he can sleep again. Half an hour of his time could save the company he's spent fifty years building. Your sisters are hooligans. The police want to question them about a man who committed suicide, the comedian Peter Walker."

"Oh, God," said Florence. "He committed suicide? But they had him under observation."

"He managed to hang himself in the shower," said Chris. "He took the flex from his television and hid it around his waist."

"I guess there's always a way if you're determined enough," said Wilson. "For our purposes, one of the reasons to get the lawyers to meet us in London is to create a conflict of interest with your sisters. If we ask Braggs to make a case against Megan and Abigail for conspiring with Dr. Bob to imprison your father in Meadowmeade, then they can't represent your sisters in the matter of Walker's suicide, since I have presented Walker as a friend who tried to help your father escape. When two parties are in conflict, the ones to employ the lawyers first can exclude the others from being represented by the same firm."

"What if Meg and Abby have already spoken to them?" asked Florence.

"They haven't and now they can't. I've made a preliminary request."

"Well, if that's already taken care of, why do we have to go to London?"

"There are still certain documents," said Wilson, "that are lodged in London: a will for all his non-Trust property that could be changed in your favor. The Trust is incorporated in Delaware, but for historic reasons he made his private will over here."

"I don't want his property; I just want him to get

well," said Florence. "Anyhow, I don't think the lawyers are going to agree to change anything in his current state."

"Exactly," said Wilson. "It's a win–win: if we get what we appear to want, it will be to our advantage. We can change the will and get you a power of attorney, but if Braggs refuses to give it, we will insist on a document declaring that Henry is not of sound mind. I can use that to raise the question of whether he was fit to give away his power in the first place, and if he was fit, why he was put in a psychiatric clinic. In other words, I can make trouble and buy time for him to recover. I have allies on the Board who will insist that I come to the meeting if I can get that document."

"So, we don't really want what we're asking for?"

"That's the beauty of it—either result is good."

"Half an hour?" said Florence.

"That's all it should take. All the documents are ready, and we have a whole team coming: a senior partner, witnesses, and a very good American attorney to help us with the international implications—a British power of attorney won't work in the States, so he has an American one prepared. After that Henry can sleep for ten hours and wake up in New York and it'll still be Tuesday evening. He can have two more nights of rest before the meeting."

"Okay, let's do it," said Florence.

"Shall I tell the pilot that we're ready to go?" asked Chris.

"Go ahead," said Florence. "I'm just going to sit with my father during the flight, in case he wakes up."

Florence went into Dunbar's bedroom, where she found the doctor standing at the foot of the bed with folded arms.

"Oh, hello," he said. "He's getting some sleep. The food rather knocked him out, after not sleeping for so long. I expect you'd like to be alone with him."

"Yes, please," said Florence. "Anyway, you should get a seat, we're going to leave as soon as possible."

Florence stretched out on the bed beside her father, ready to hold him in case the take-off disturbed his rest. The plane accelerated along the runway and made its steep and rapid ascent out of Manchester. Once its flight path flattened out, Florence sat up cross-legged, resting against the gray leather bedhead with a pillow in the small of her back. She looked down on her father's face and realized that she had almost never seen it from above. In her eyes, he had always been towering over everyone. She had once been to visit him in Los Angeles when he was ill, but she had almost immediately, instinctively sat down in a chair next to his high bed to restore the natural order of things, looking up at him, raised among his pillows. When she was four or five, she could remember the time he had fallen asleep, stretched out on a sofa on the verandah at Home Lake, with a book spread open on his chest, and she went over and patted his face affectionately until her mother whispered to her to come away and let her father sleep. Now, his matted white hair was longer than she had ever seen it and three days of stubble covered his usually clean-shaven jaw. He had lost weight and looked older, with the lines on his forehead and around his eyes and in his sagging cheeks more deeply grooved than before.

She had hardly been able to speak with him since she retrieved him from that barren mountainside a few hours ago. Her father had refused to wear headphones on the helicopter, indeed he had recoiled from them, clutching his head, as if he were being offered a vice or some other instrument of torture. She decided to take the helicopter straight to Manchester airport, with Mark and Wilson following with the luggage by car. Although he mumbled to himself throughout the journey, what he said was inaudible, and what she was saying to Chris and the helicopter pilot was inaudible to him, which was just as well, since she was emphasizing the importance of landing on the far side of her plane in order to block the view of Global One. Her plane was parked as far away as possible, but there was nowhere on the tarmac from which Dunbar's big old Boeing could not be seen, unless something was in the way. Global One had always been her father's favorite toy. It was like another home to him, a home with no fixed address, decorated to his specifications; its astonishing paneled library, carpeted with a pale gold Persian rug, had still lifes by Chardin and William Nicholson hanging between the bookshelves. As a child, the room that amazed her most was the hammam, where she had watched the orange, green, and black geometric tiles on the walls and benches fade among clouds of steam, knowing that the plane was floating thirty thousand feet above the glaciers of Greenland or the deserts of New Mexico.

Florence thought that seeing his old plane and not being allowed on board would throw her father into a deeper turmoil, but once he was safely installed in her rented Gulfstream, she wondered if it would have made such a difference after all. Perhaps she had been trying to protect him from a confusion that he had already exceeded long ago. He seemed to be bewildered by simply being on a plane. He asked continually if Simon was safe and whether Peter had made it to London. She hadn't known at the time that Peter was dead, nor had she said that he was at Meadowmeade because her father seemed so desperate to see him again. When she asked who Simon was, all Dunbar could say was that he was a religious man who had saved his life and that they must make sure that he was all right and to "put him on the payroll." He seemed to recognize Florence as a beneficent figure who had found him when he was lost, but if he understood their relationship, he kept forgetting what it was.

Dunbar's mumbling anxiety about the fate of the two men who had helped him to escape only yielded to other emotions when Wilson and Mark turned up by car an hour later. He stared at Wilson with an expression of irresolute intensity, trying to place the face, coming up with a theory and then seeming to dismiss it as altogether too improbable.

Mark, on the other hand, produced a reaction of instant rage.

"You! You!" shouted Dunbar, pointing at his sleek and slightly corpulent son-in-law. "No! Not you! Get him out of here! He has conspired against me and had me locked away. You can't make me go back!" and with these words he leapt out of his chair and dashed with surprising alacrity down the corridor of the plane and locked himself in one of the bedrooms.

Wilson and Florence had no hesitation in asking Mark to go back to New York on another plane. Florence had the impression that Mark was more put out by the prospect of taking a commercial flight than he was by the way her father had responded to his arrival.

"Of course," he said, with a tattered version of his habitual suavity. "Henry seems to be in a thoroughly confused state, poor man. I hope you'll put him right about my role and explain that it was precisely my strong objection to his imprisonment that got me over here in the first place."

While the doctor busied himself with his stethoscope and his blood pressure monitor, his torch and his reflex hammer, Dunbar slipped into an abstracted state, as if he were looking at a screen behind his eyes on which an alternative story was being projected. Florence felt that the plane, the plans, and all the people around him were not radically absent in his mind but, like the Exit signs in a darkened cinema, they couldn't be expected to compete with something as absorbing as the film itself. After eating some chicken soup and some bread he fell asleep almost immediately.

Sitting beside him with a hand resting lightly on his shoulder, Florence felt relieved to have her father under her protection, but disturbed by the thought that the person she yearned to be reconciled with might never return from the mental exile he had been driven to by her sisters. She had flown into the Cumbrian wilderness to fetch him, but she had no idea how to retrieve him from the wilderness of his psyche. Nothing in his ascent to power had prepared him for the experience of the last weeks and in particular of the last few days, which seemed to have overrun his mind with a kind of knowledge that he was unable to make sense of. Like a deluge rushing onto a flat, rocky plain, with no slope to direct it or soil to absorb it, it had obliterated all familiar landmarks without bringing any new life in return. How could she reach him in the middle of that sterile flood?

As the plane hit a band of turbulence on its way down to London, Dunbar frowned in his sleep and then half opened his eyes. He looked up at Florence's face with an incredulity verging on resentment.

"Has anyone told you that you look like my youngest daughter?" he asked, speaking with unexpected clarity, given the state he had been in before he fell asleep.

"I am your daughter," she said. "I'm Florence."

"No," said Dunbar. "You can't be, but it's true that you do look like her."

He raised his hands, bracketing the air around his head.

"I've been having trouble," he said, his fingers testing the space, as if he were trying to locate the extent of a bruise, "getting my thoughts in order."

"Yes," said Florence.

"When you mustn't walk on the cracks between the paving stones, but you can't walk anywhere else . . ." he paused, his fingers continuing to explore, like a blind man reading a face, ". . . and the thing that you must avoid at all costs is the only thing that happens."

"I understand," said Florence, "but you're safe now."

"Safe?" said Dunbar bitterly. "If you think that, you're a fool. Being alive is falling, once you know that, it never stops. Do you understand what I'm telling you? There is no ground, nothing to catch you . . ."

Florence could feel what he was saying, but could think of no way to respond. There was no point in trying to argue a person out of a feeling, and in the case of this particular feeling, that nothing was safe, reassurance would only sound like another argument in disguise. He seemed to have become more lucid after a little food and a little rest, but only in order to describe his confusion and his despair more lucidly. All she could do was to stay with him and to wish him well.

"What's that?" said Dunbar, startled by the plane's slightly bumpy landing.

"We've arrived in London," said Florence.

"Is Peter here?" asked Dunbar anxiously.

"No, he stayed behind in Cumbria."

"Silly fool," said Dunbar, "we were going to go to Rome to drink Negronis, that's what he said, among some of the most beautiful ruins in the world. He helped me to escape from the prison camp. We must put him on the payroll."

"We will, Daddy," said Florence, getting off the bed in preparation for the visitors her father would soon be receiving. She felt she should not be present when legal documents might be changed in her favor. It might seem like a subtle form of coercion, and besides the team that Wilson described wouldn't be able to fit in her father's room, even without her being there as well.

"What did you call me?" said Dunbar, "Florence, is that you?"

"Yes," said Florence.

"I've been looking for you everywhere," said Dunbar, holding his arms out.

Florence moved round to the far side of the bed and knelt down beside her father, kissing him on either cheek.

He reached out and tentatively touched the top of her head.

"Can you ever forgive me?" he said, "cutting you and your children off and giving everything to those two monsters? I have been proud and tyrannical and, worst of all, stupid."

Florence looked up and saw that her father's face was soaked in tears.

"Of course, of course," she said, "I'm the one who has been proud. I should have made the first move long ago."

"No," Dunbar insisted, "it was my wretched temper

that caused the trouble, and the habit of being in command. Ha!" he let out a short guffaw, full of disillusion. "I can't even command—sometimes I reach the end of a thought and I have already forgotten where it started."

"Well, we're never going to fall out again," said Florence, kissing her father's forehead and briefly resting her head on his chest.

"Never again," said Dunbar, holding her face tenderly in both his hands. "My darling Catherine," he said, shaking his head in disbelief, "I thought I'd lost you, but you're alive."

14

In the confusion and despondency that followed Florence's success, Megan was experiencing one of those rare moments in which she wished her husband hadn't died so unexpectedly last year. By the time she met him, Victor Allen's colorful Wall Street career had already earned him the nickname "Mad Dog"; in the last ten years of their marriage he had been promoted to "Evil Fuck." No major deal could take place, even ones that Victor had never glanced at, without the question, "Where is Evil Fuck on this one?" being voiced in anxious conference rooms around the world. He took considerable pride in turning what might have been a pathetically vague description, applicable to any number of his colleagues, into a personal title. In a world in which his rivals tended to be known as Darth Vader, Lord Sauron, or Voldemort, Victor also regarded his sobriquet as a sign of maturity, made up as it was of two plain English words, without any cute allusions to children's entertainment. Generally speaking, he was a man exhilarated by insults, just as he was impatient of praise, which he regarded as either "a blinding statement of the obvious" or a Trojan horse for extracting money from him. It was hard to point to any particular deal or innovation that justified the title he grew to cherish: his exploitation of barely legal tax loopholes, his creation of catastrophic debt, using ever more intricate and deceptive financial instruments, his preparedness to rip apart old and successful companies, on which whole communities and tens of thousands of families depended, in order to make a few investors even more disruptively rich, were in themselves no more surprising on Wall Street than finding bread in a bakery, but the scale of his operations, the extent of his duplicity, and the intensity of his sarcasm and triumphalism meant that, like a runner who still has the reserves to sprint at the end of a marathon, he broke away from the bobbing mass of evil fucks in his generation and crossed the finish line ahead of the competition.

If only he were still around, or, even better, if only he could come back for a week, like a special guest star in a hot television series, and then disappear again. It had been tough for Megan to line up enough eulogies at Victor's memorial service to do justice to her status as a very important widow, but right now she could almost have written a poem for that impoverished occasion. As Jesus busied himself trying to bring her to orgasm, she started to imagine the first line. "Victor, thou shouldst be living at this hour!" That was a firm traditional start . . . "We need thy venom and thy debt . . ." She couldn't immediately think of anything that rhymed with "debt," but in any case, the inspiration for her poem was the fact that Victor would have improvised some wonderfully aggressive or devious move to secure the buyout of the Dunbar Trust. His old partner, Dick Bild, was holding the line, but could he be trusted to go to the necessary extremes?

Oh, that was an unexpected little thrill! Jesus had managed to capture her attention. There was no doubt that he deserved an "A" for effort and he was certainly making better use of his tongue than when he murmured inane compliments from a neighboring pillow, showing her that he was not just a ruthless killer but a bashful little boy who allowed his mother's tender Hispanic influence, already quite conspicuous enough in his Christian name, to give a sibilant softness to a Texan accent otherwise hardened and whitewashed by his belt-wielding, truck-driving, hard-drinking, dreadful old ex-military Pa. She already knew the whole dreary story.

She realized she hadn't sighed for ages. She probably should, or perhaps even moan.

"Don't stop," she said, catching her breath, "please don't stop."

If he stopped, he might talk. On balance, she was better off as she was, although it was tempting to scream with frustration, while thrashing about to give the impression that she was in an epileptic sexual ecstasy.

Of course one had to be prepared to run into occasional patches of turbulence, but the last few hours had been really ridiculous. The British police, who wanted to question her team about Peter Walker's suicide, had almost caught up with them, but they had just managed to get Global One off the ground in time. A few minutes later and they would have been in some godawful provincial police station. And then Braggs had started behaving strangely, saying it couldn't represent them in this particular case, due to a conflict of interest. Obviously, Dr. Harris was more of a wily old fox than he seemed at first sight. In any case her conscience was clear: how were they supposed to be responsible, when they were miles away at the time, for a complete lunatic hanging himself in an asylum shower? She wasn't surprised that they were being accused; people never tired of attacking her family. It was envy, of course, pure and simple. There was nothing one could do about envy, it was just part of human nature; her mother had warned her about it on her first day of kindergarten, but it was especially disappointing to see it rear its ugly head at this precise moment.

Florence had been a complete nightmare as usual. They had managed to get rid of her for a year, but now she had come back in order to meddle in things that she knew nothing about. Of course she had been the one to get Daddy, as she always had been. The last daughter to arrive, she was still the first to have really captured his attention. Through most of Megan's life, Florence had sat there smugly monopolizing their father's love, while no amount of obedience, flattery, or aping of his attitudes could secure a single drop for either of her sisters. This time it was too serious to let Florence get away with being Daddy's little favorite. Florence now stood between Megan and the prize that she and Abby had been working toward for three years. Bloated on her father's love, she was like a grazing cow that wanders onto the railway tracks just as a high-speed train is coming round the bend. As far as Megan was concerned, the consequences were inevitable.

Florence would of course claim that her sudden presence was entirely motivated by concern for their father but, first of all, he had been in an excellent (and very expensive) facility where he was being given the best professional care and, secondly, he was not just any old doddery father who needed to be visited in his nursing home (which she had fully intended to do in due course), but a powerful symbol around whom all sorts of outdated and reactionary forces might gather. She and Abigail had been secretly cultivating the least self-righteous directors, offering them not entirely ethical inducements to favor Eagle Rock's bid. They hadn't dared approach Dunbar and Wilson's old allies, but with their own votes and with Dr. Bob joining the Board, they expected to command a slim majority, hoping the rest of the directors would be brought around by the very generous proposal itself.

Eagle Rock would be offering fifteen percent over the current share price, making it a bonanza for ordinary shareholders. It would of course be quite wrong to pile a huge burden of debt on the poor Trust: it was, after all, excessive debts that led to massive redundancies, fire sales of subsidiaries, and the destruction of fine old companies. In other words, exactly what they had in mind! They were going to make the Trust leaner and meaner, and then make a new public offering of the streamlined company five years down the road. According to Dick Bild, she and Abby could expect to make 1.4 billion dollars each—which didn't seem that much, considering what a pain it was turning out to be—but they were only doing what made sound business sense, and it was better to have it done by people who truly loved the company and not by some rapacious outsider. Really, there was nothing to worry about. Eagle Rock had a very clear, fully financed, legally bulletproof friendly merger proposal, and nobody else would be interested in the Dunbar Trust at this price since it had lost the China satellite deal to Unicom.

"Oh God, that feels good," she groaned.

It was quite frightening how soon she tired of her lovers. J had seemed so thrilling last night, with his glowing young body, and his look of feverish concentration, worthy of a man working against the clock to defuse a nuclear device but all in fact lavished on bringing her wave after wave of pleasure. How could he already feel like a misguided revival? It couldn't just be that Dr. Bob was no longer in the room next door, making it less fun to abandon herself to fits of amplified screaming. She wasn't that superficial, although there had been a certain vindictive comfort in knowing that he was on the other side of the wall, seething with jealousy, or at least insomnia. In a better world than this, J might have lasted a few weeks, or just stuck around as a sexual opportunity she took up when it suited her, but the pressure of the times meant that she was going to have to ask him for a special favor. She wouldn't have time to dress up the request, except to give it an air of heart-wrenching necessity. She would shed silent but copious tears, genuinely impressed by the burden placed on her in having to ask something so unnatural, but also intuiting that J would be powerless in the face of her tears, having spent much of his violent childhood comforting his beaten mother as she wept in a corner of their bungalow. J would assent with fitting gravity, while advancing the theory that in his opinion it took real courage on her part to make such a tough decision. She would respond by clinging to him more tightly and squeezing a little more fluid from her tear ducts onto his hairless chest. In a moment of pure stillness, a small puddle might form between his intimidating pectorals. Megan couldn't help being impressed by her own painstaking choreography.

Perhaps that was the trouble: now that she had imagined J being launched, like a heat-seeking missile, it seemed counterintuitive, not to say hazardous, to keep hanging on to him. And yet she knew that this particular crash in erotic enthusiasm was only a detail in the pattern. Her lovers slept beside a precipice that seemed to move closer with each affair. Would the coastal erosion ever stop? Would it go on until she

fell over the edge as well and joined the litter of broken bodies on the beach?

Love was all theater of course. She was the eternally
dissatisfied director, as well as the star around whom
the whole production was built. If the leading man
got fired for some reason, there was always an under-
study to take his place. Essentially, no one else in the
cast mattered. There was no autonomous reason for
their existence. They were multiples of zero. She could
remember having her one and only Maths epiphany
when she was ten, realizing that adding a zero to the
end of a figure multiplied it tenfold, but multiplying
a figure, however large, by zero, nullified it. That was
why she preferred to think of a person as a multiple of
zero rather than "a complete zero," given the radically
different roles played by that naughty nought in different contexts.

In J's case, the relationship was going to be especially brief, since it wouldn't be expedient to be seen
with him after he had performed his little service
for her; in fact, sadly enough, Kevin might have to
eliminate the danger of any traces that could lead
back to her. The trouble with getting people to eliminate traces was that they became a trace in their own
right. Who eliminates the eliminator? There had been
a time—she had never told anyone about it, and even
in private it was a memory she resisted having—when
she was capable of taking the initiative all on her own.
Thank God the crash was bad enough to destroy all
evidence of tampering. She had been so young and

so merciless. All the bad things she'd done since had some sort of worldly pretext, but that had been an act of pure hatred. Although it had taken some time to organize, it had somehow remained impulsive, in the sense that her hatred renewed itself so forcefully that it never allowed a moment of reflection. Part of her was still a little shocked by what she had done all those years ago and didn't want to dwell on it too long. It was so unsophisticated to be shocked by things.

Judging that it was probably time for the big scream, Megan started to gasp and to tense her body. She found herself enjoying the sensation of having J's head clamped firmly between her thighs and started to arch her back and tighten her grip. She couldn't help thinking that he probably hadn't been in such a vulnerable position since his personal combat training at the Green Beret Center for Martial Arts Excellence. Maybe if she twisted suddenly enough, she could just snap his neck and kick his limp body onto the floor. She found herself irresistibly drawn to that prospect. There she was, about to produce the fakest orgasm of all time, but now there was no doubt that she was getting really worked up by her little fantasy.

"Oh, my God," she said, imagining the sound of his snapping neck, "Oh, my God."

She clenched her thighs harder and rose higher off the bed. One simple, sudden twist, that's all it would take.

"Oh, my God . . . I'm coming!" she gasped, with genuine astonishment.

J hoisted himself up, crawled along beside her still trembling body and collapsed next to her, gently massaging his neck.

"You sure got strong thighs," he remarked, admiringly.

"Oh, J, you're an artist," said Megan. "I can't tell you how you inspired me."

"It's only because I'm so inspired by you, querida," said J, looking foolishly pleased.

His lisping endearment and his devoted expression instantly irritated Megan.

"Oh, J," she said, "I haven't come so hard since, well, since last night." She smiled, grazing his rib cage with her fingernails.

"Querida, I want to hold you all night in my arms," said the besotted warrior.

"Hold me, hold me," said Megan.

"I don't know if this is just a regular thing for you," said J, "but I don't think I've ever really been in love before."

"That's such a sweet thing to say," she said. "Of course it's not a regular thing for me. I'm completely dazzled by how strong it all feels."

She kissed his chest, managing to extort a small tear from one eye that, after an annoyingly long journey down the side of her nose, finally dripped onto its target.

"Querida!" said the hypersensitive J, devastated that the woman he was holding in his arms, his woman, was crying. "Que passa?"

"Oh, it's nothing," said Megan bravely.

Hearing her own fortitude filled her with self-pity and released another precious tear. She plunged into the feeling with all the method at her command— she had done two semesters at the Lee Strasberg Institute before dropping out. She closed her eyes and tried to picture the sorrows that were afflicting her. Just when she had found a sexual fantasy that really worked for her, she was having it taken away. She knew that it wasn't randomly transferable, but intimately tied up with J being a soldier, with the feeling of having a killer in her power, of having fatally weakened a man enchanted by his own physical strength. All the more reason not to fall into the Delilah Trap, thought Megan, straying from her purpose and returning to more familiar calculations, and leave Samson chained to a couple of blackmailing pillars, ready to bring the whole edifice of her life crashing down around her. After he had done what had to be done, J would have to go. Maybe they could do it one more time; it was only Tuesday, after all. Yes, that would work, one more time tonight in the city and maybe one more time before breakfast. Then she would let go of him. A missile was the exemplary multiple of zero: once it hit the target it ceased to exist. Thanks to Mark, they were a step ahead of their rivals. He had given them all sorts of useful information when he climbed on board Global One, saving them hours of research. His explanation for being in Manchester was completely unconvincing, but after flirting with the enemy, he had obviously decided that his real interests ultimately lay with his wife. He had overheard that Florence was planning to disinherit her own sisters of all the non-Trust property. Greedy bitch.

All these misfortunes: Florence's manhunting triumph and appropriation of all their father's personal property; her own loss of a lover to the higher purpose of a total victory over her loathsome half-sister and, above all, the cumulative burden of always having to be strong and sharp and in charge and one step ahead, suddenly engendered the breakdown she had been straining to achieve. Her eyes streamed, and her trembling, sobbing body clung ever more tightly to her protector. She had gone to see a therapist once who irritated her so much that she had quit almost immediately. He used to interrupt what she thought were rather amusing anecdotes, giving him a glimpse of a world that he would never have access to in his own right, by saying things like, "And where is little Megan at this glitzy party? Where is she hiding?" Now, unexpectedly, his voice and his ridiculous questions came back to her and she let out a wail of real pain.

J was completely helpless, as Megan had imagined he would be, holding the weeping body of the woman he loved.

"Querida, please," he pleaded. "I will do anything to stop you crying. Just tell me what is wrong."

Megan sobbed a little longer and then sat up, reached for the box of handkerchiefs beside the bed and blew her nose.

She put her head back on J's shoulder, and continued to cry more quietly. She had found little Megan now, hiding in the cupboard, and when she spoke it was in the strangely young voice of a frightened, distrustful child.

"Anything?" she whispered.

"Anything," said J. "I swear, anything at all."

15

By the time Florence's plane landed in New York, everyone on board was in a state of tension and uncertainty, except for Dunbar, who was profoundly asleep, resting for the first time in days and safe for the first time in weeks. The papers had all been duly signed with Braggs in London and there was nothing more to do for the moment. Florence decided to wait until her father woke up naturally, letting Chris and Wilson go ahead to their hotel. They agreed to meet on Wednesday morning to discuss their strategy for the following day and for Dunbar to reinstate Wilson as his counsel, if he chose to. While Chris and Wilson were driven by a desire to take back control of the company, Florence was divided between following them to a deserved but doubtful victory and completely protecting her father by taking him back home with her to Wyoming. She felt that what he needed was a deeper renunciation of power, not a restoration to power. Why not just take the plane on, and leave

Wilson and Chris to fight for justice on their own? Why should her battered father be dragged through another corporate battle?

Florence waited patiently on the plane. She knew that the jet rental company would happily provide another pilot and co-pilot and that she could probably take her father home in time for breakfast and immerse him in an atmosphere of calm and love. She could give him a room with a big log fire burning in the grate and wide windows looking out on to mind-emptying views of silent fields and snowy woods, all contained by a parapet of distant mountains; a scene more likely to heal his mind than a stack of binders filled with bar charts, legal arguments, and spreadsheets. And yet, it was not her decision to make. Even if her intentions were the opposite of her sisters," her methods could not be the same. She could not abduct her father, even to heal him. She must ask him, when he finally woke, what he wanted to do.

Abby was more disturbed by the police inquiry into Peter Walker's suicide than she had been prepared to show. In fact she had been close to panic while she waited for Global One to take off. During that agonizing delay, she toyed with the idea of blaming herself for the intemperance of pulling the trigger on that silly lighter and precipitating all these international complications, but as the plane reached its cruising altitude somewhere over Irish airspace she realized, with a rush of indignation, that Walker had in fact been asking for his punishment by behaving in such a pusillanimous way. It was almost an act of kindness to set him alight, showing him that his terror of being burnt was much worse than the reality of being wrapped for a few seconds in a mantle of blue flame, like a baked Alaska, or a Christmas pudding. A normal person would have snapped out of it, or fought back, but Walker was a neurotic mess, a man who'd made a living out of having no idea who he was. What could one expect from such a degenerate specimen?

Although the allegations against her were clearly ridiculous, it was important to prepare some kind of defense. The key was to agree on a story and to enforce it. Notwithstanding her little sister's rather blatant crush on Kevin's latest recruit, it was obvious that Jesus would have to take the fall. She couldn't sacrifice Dr. Bob, who was about to become a director of the Trust, and it was easier to keep Kevin, who'd been with her for years.

Yes, that's what had happened: against their collective pleas, J had set light to the hapless comedian, not burning him at all seriously, but certainly acting overzealously to make sure that Walker was telling the truth. In his defense, they had all been beside themselves with worry about her aged father facing almost certain death as he wandered through the snowy wastes of Cumbria, lured by a sad combination of his own confusion, Meadowmeade's breathtaking incompetence, and Walker's pernicious addiction to alcohol. If J—at this point Dr. Bob could testify that Jesus was suffering from post-traumatic stress syn-

drome after his heroic service in Iraq, and had actually mistaken Walker for an insurgent in a terrifying
flashback to an episode of barbaric torture inflicted
on him in the backstreets of Baghdad—would agree
to pay his debt to society and spend a couple of years
in prison, several million dollars would be waiting for
him on his release. The more Abby thought about it,
the more she calmed down. It was normally the kind
of crisis she would have dealt with in her sleep, but the
whole thing had been blown out of proportion by the
tension surrounding the privatization of the Trust.

She was generally cheered up by the thought of
what money could do. If the death of nature could be
monetized in the form of carbon tax and a lively trade
in pollution credits, what on earth had made her
imagine there wasn't a financial solution to a silly old
private suicide? It just showed how stressed she was at
the moment. She really owed it to herself, when this
was all over, to take a month off in Canyon Ranch,
even if it meant rescheduling the spring.

"You're still in love with her, aren't you?" said Wilson.

"Yup," said Chris, "no end in sight."

Their car turned onto Madison Avenue and began
its run uptown through a gauntlet of shops glowing
luxuriously in the winter darkness. Chris was already
missing Florence. She would always be the woman he
loved without reservation: the one he loved *and* liked,
the one he'd be proud to go out with and happy to stay
home with, the one who was exciting and reassuring

at the same time. They had been together all the time over the last few days and although they were due to meet the next morning, that phase of the journey was over. She would be in her apartment tonight and soon enough back home with her family. On the way over from London, in what had felt like a last chance to have an intimate conversation, they congratulated each other on their restraint, with a mixture of humor and regret that showed how close they had come to abandoning it. Agreeing on how wise they had been only made him long for her more than ever. Chris felt that they were entitled to kiss as a reward for the self-control they had shown in not having kissed already. In fact, given how well they had behaved, they might as well move in together and have some children. If it was so painful and confusing doing the right thing, why not do the wrong thing instead? He had some-how contrived to feel the stab of a breakup without having had the joy of a reunion.

"Part of me thinks that this latest wave of love is tied up with her unavailability," said Chris. "When we actually lived together, we broke up every few months."

"Sometimes, it seemed like every few hours," said Wilson. "I remember going on a trip to China with Henry and when we got back we said, 'Gee, the kids are still together!' It turned out you'd broken up and got back together while we were away."

"Sure," said Chris, "but it's different now."

He paused to remind himself of the irony and fu-tility of getting on so well with a happily married

ex-girlfriend with two children and a kind and quietly impressive husband. He was relieved when the
car turned down 76th Street and stopped outside the
entrance of the hotel. He longed to disperse his mel-
ancholy in the bustle and practicality of arrival.

"Who knows?" said Chris.

Wilson reached out and touched his forearm in silent solidarity.

Dr. Bob had insisted on having a car of his own to
pick him up at the airport. He urgently needed to talk
with Steve Cogniccenti. A good deal of planning had
gone into even scheduling the call. They were going
to speak at 11:15, by which time Steve would be on his
way home after a dinner he was attending without his
wife, alone in the back of his car, partitioned from
the driver, ready to give Dr. Bob up to fifteen minutes of his attention. Dr. Bob had ordered a proper old
stretch limo so as to be partitioned as well. When he
arrived on Global One he usually caught a free ride,
or at least ordered a normal car that looked as if it was
designed to carry half a platoon of marines through
the war-torn streets of Mogadishu, rather than something from a documentary about the history of rock
music, but fortunately his fellow travelers were too
preoccupied to notice or comment.

Although he had dozed for a couple of hours on
the plane, he was so profoundly exhausted by the last
week that he was beyond stimulation. With any luck
once he got back to his apartment he would collapse

completely, sleep for ten hours, and then hit the Adderall the next morning with some effect. He might sound stupefied to Steve, but there was only one major piece of news to communicate: Dunbar was back in play.

Since it was 11:02 and Steve was fanatically punctual, Dr. Bob allowed himself to close his eyes and to rest his mind. He could think of nothing that he ought to be thinking about, which was just as well, given that he couldn't think at all. For the last week he had been unable to stop thinking; now he had hit a wall and couldn't begin to formulate a thought.

Shit! He must have fallen asleep. Where was he? He stared bemusedly at the cheap cell phone squawking in the black leather seat beside him. Then he remembered what he was supposed to be doing and grabbed it greedily.

"Steve!" he said, rather too loudly and suddenly.

"Bob! What happened? You fell asleep, right? I was about to hang up."

"No, not at all," said Dr. Bob, "I only just got in the car and had to get the phone out of my bag. We landed a little later than expected."

Dr. Bob wondered why he was bothering to lie. He was a much more abstemious liar than the Dunbar sisters, feeling that unnecessary lies just multiplied the danger of discovery. He normally would have admitted to falling asleep, but Cogniccenti created an atmosphere of paranoia. Despite his specious bonhomie he gave the impression of perpetually searching for weakness, like a polar bear pounding the ice to dig out a seal cub nesting under the surface.

"How was Austria?" said Steve. "Have you got the old man in a secure facility with Alsatians patrolling the perimeter?"

"Well, that didn't pan out quite the way we planned it," said Dr. Bob, immediately feeling defensive and wondering if there was any way Cogniccenti could take his money back.

"How so?"

"Florence got to her father before we could and she's brought him back here."

"This is a fuck-up, Bob," said Steve coldly. "This is not what we agreed. Dunbar is one of the toughest negotiators on the planet; we needed to get him out of the picture. Is he going to be in any shape to attend their meeting on Thursday?"

"Absolutely not," said Dr. Bob. "He was lost in a storm in the Lake District for the best part of three days, with nothing to eat and nowhere to sleep. It's a wonder he's alive at all. Mark Rush saw him earlier today and said that he's completely incoherent and physically wrecked. I'm sorry we couldn't secure him. Florence got the police involved—"

"I'm not interested in what happened," Steve interrupted. "I'm only looking in one direction: straight ahead. After this call, I want you to destroy the phone you're using right now. I'm going to do the same with mine."

"But how will I get hold of you?"

"You won't. This is our last conversation until the takeover is completed. Then we can meet up to celebrate."

"Okay," said Dr. Bob, who'd never heard anyone who sounded less inclined to celebrate with him. Before he could say anything to round off the conversation amicably, he realized that the connection had gone dead.

"Well, fuck you, too," he muttered, lowering the tinted window to his right and posting his Unicom phone into four lanes of busy traffic on the highway.

Like a swimmer blowing the water from his flooded snorkel before returning to the reassuring, amplified rhythm of his breathing, Dunbar threw off the weight of his dream; the dream of a stag being pursued by dogs and men intent on bursting his heart. He emerged at a level where he could hear his own labored breath and knew that he had been dreaming, but without being fully awake and without knowing where he was. His mind was a bruise of pure emotion with no conscious direction or sense of context. Each pulse of fear and longing and hope was like an overdose pushing him back into a dream. He pictured himself trying to clamber out of a rough sea onto a rocky shore, and being reclaimed again and again by an indisputable wave that dragged him back out into the open water. He woke a little more on his next attempt. The sharp rocks of his half-dream cut into his bare feet and hands as he scrambled to get beyond the reach of the exploding waves. He felt the sting of his lacerated skin and, as he emerged further, into a more rational realm, the image of the seashore receded and disappeared. His confusion no longer took the form of overpowering visions, but of unanswerable arguments. He had a memory of seeing Catherine recently, which he knew must be false, unless he was dead, which he did not believe to be the case. So what the hell was going on?

He opened his eyes. He was definitely not dead, unless death was a perfect replica of life. Perhaps the dead were removed, like sculptures that are buried in museums to protect them from curious crowds and acid rain, and then replaced by the copies that preside over public squares and excavated cities. Anything seemed possible on these contested borders, but what were they the borders between: life and death, or sanity and madness? He couldn't tell what was private anymore.

"Hello," he called out quietly, not knowing whether he was inviting help or hurt. And then he called more loudly, because the pain of not knowing what was going on was even greater than the possibility of things going wrong.

"Hello!"

The door opened and a lovely woman came into the room. Dunbar's immediate past, which had been hidden by dreams and speculations, suddenly fell into place.

"Florence," he said, "it's you."

"Yes, Daddy."

"You saved me when I was lost."

Florence came over and sat on the edge of the bed by her father and instinctively reached out and brushed some of the hair from his forehead, and rested her hand on the side of his face, as she would have if one of her children were suffering from a fever. Dunbar reached up and covered her hand with his own. He had been so starved of gentleness that tears swelled up spontaneously in his eyes.

"We were on a plane to London," he said.

"That's right, and now we've flown on to New York."

"New York," said Dunbar, like someone who had heard about it but never imagined he would go there.

"I was waiting for you to wake up and then I thought we could go to my apartment in the city, if you like, or," Florence hesitated, "we could go back to my place in Wyoming. You've never been there before, but it's really cosy and the land around is very beautiful."

"No more land," said Dunbar.

"You'd be looking at it from a safe place," said Florence, "not lost in it."

"No more land," said Dunbar firmly. "Don't I have a meeting to go to? Wilson was here and he said there was a meeting."

"You only have to go if you want to. The main thing is for you to get some rest."

"I've had some rest," said Dunbar, hoisting himself up on his pillows. "What time is it?"

"It's two-thirty on Wednesday morning," said Florence, half pleased and half alarmed to see the return of her father's old habit of authority. "Nobody is awake, apart from us, and so there's nothing to do except go home and settle in."

Dunbar subsided again, as if he had been told to stand at ease after making an especially rigid and formal salute.

"Nothing to do," he said, his tears working their way through the folds and ridges of his cheeks. The phrase seemed to reprieve him for a while from a world of suffering, but he couldn't stay away for long.

"Can you forgive me?" He asked. "I've been so confused, not just recently but always—"

"There's nothing to forgive," she interrupted him.

"This is what matters," he said, pressing her hand.

"We can just leave," said Florence; "if this is what matters, let's just go away and forget about the meeting."

"But it's all part of it," said Dunbar, caught up again. "I mustn't let your sisters take the Trust. I want it to go to you and your children."

"We're fine," said Florence, "we've got enough."

"Enough," said Dunbar, amazed again. "You've got enough and there's nothing to do." He let these two simple phrases shine for a moment, like a man holding a gem to the light to see if it has any hidden flaws, but then, as if he had never really meant to buy them in the first place, he returned them to Florence with a shake of the head.

"They mustn't be allowed to get away with it," he said.

"It's just how they are," said Florence. "Let them have it."

"No," said Dunbar. "It's the legacy."

16

It was five in the morning when Jesus walked out through the checkered marble hall of Megan's building, past the half-sleepy and half-contemptuous night porter who thought he knew exactly what was going on, and had no intention of opening the door for Mrs. Allen's latest "personal trainer."

Park Avenue was dark and unseasonably warm. Cabs drifted by, but J was in the mood to walk, to stay focused on this incredible feeling that was expanding inside him. He was in love for the first time in his life, truly in love. He wanted to surrender to Megan completely, to merge with her, to be an extension of her will. He hadn't abandoned himself to another person since he was a tiny kid and naturally loved his mom with all his heart, but then instead of looking after him, she had needed his protection and his comforting. Of course he would protect Megan on a security level, but in the bigger picture she was the magic woman he had always wanted, the woman who was going to totally look after him. She said they were going to live together, that she wanted him around her all the time, because he made her feel safe and excited all at once, which was every woman's dream. After he had done the "special favor" she had requested she was going to take him to her place in Maui, "a real paradise on Earth." She had shown him photographs of the vast white house on top of a Hawaiian hill, with a path leading down to a private beach, and mangos you could just reach up and pluck off a tree. And while he looked at the pictures, he had this movie running in his head, thinking of all the ways he was going to drive her crazy with desire, but then he had recoiled from his own porno fantasies, because it was so much more than a sex thing: it was a total thing, as if they were one person. Just being separated from her right now felt like being punched with his hands tied. They were meant to be together, totally together all the time.

He wasn't going to let anything steal his attention from this beautiful feeling. Everything else could be delegated to his inner drill sergeant, a cold bastard who got things done without wasting his time having feelings about what he was doing. If somebody needed to be taught a lesson, he was the man. If somebody needed to have the fear of God put into her soul, the sergeant was on it. Just say the word. No problem. Job done.

————

Mark was not exactly proud of what he'd done, but his overall pride, like a large, diversified portfolio, could easily survive the crash of an individual stock, or the shame of an individual incident. Besides, was it really so shameful to catch a lift home on the family plane? There had been an odd atmosphere at the time, as he hurried over from Florence's rented jet to what might be seen as the enemy camp, but the more he thought about it on the flight over, the more he realized that he was essentially a neutral nation, a Switzerland, looking down, with distaste and regret, but without favoritism, at the raging armies slaughtering each other incompetently on the muddy plains beyond the well-guarded and mountainous frontiers of his indifference. If there was one thing he disliked more than the way his wife had treated Dunbar, it was the way Dunbar had treated him: shaking his palsied finger and making all sorts of unjustified accusations in front of everybody, in front of Wilson and his dreadful, earnest son, who was obviously desperate to get Florence, now that she was galloping back into the family business on her white charger, saving Daddy and getting all his non-Trust assets along the way. Frankly, it was all a little too sordid for his taste.

Mark sat in the cosy paneled breakfast room on the middle floor of the apartment, enjoying his tropical fruit and black coffee. He encouraged Manuela to pour him another cup of coffee and turned his attention to the Wednesday morning papers folded neatly beside him on the breakfast table. However things turned out in the end, neutrality was the order of the day. He may have paid rather too much for his ticket home by giving an exhaustive account of everything he'd found out from Florence, but from now on, when it came to keeping out of destructive conflicts, he was going to be more Swiss than the Swiss. Thank God he was seeing Mindy for lunch. She always made him feel good about himself, about who he really was and what he really stood for. She reminded him that the Rushes had been there before the Dunbars and would still be there after the Dunbars had fled the scene.

Mark picked up the *Wall Street Journal* and leafed through the first few pages of familiar headlines about low oil prices and declining Chinese stocks, eventually settling on an article that promised to reinforce his established view that government was tightening a hangman's noose of red tape around the innocent neck of the American business community. His passion for material comfort was matched by a passion for intellectual comfort, even when it took the form of indignation or, if it came to that, apocalyptic pessimism toward things he couldn't care less about, like the mounting pressure on the middle classes or the destruction of the Amazonian rainforest at the rate of one Belgium a year (or was that the melting of the Arctic ice cap?). It made him chuckle that Belgium had become a unit of ecological catastrophe, whereas in his childhood it had been used to describe the vastness of the lost estates (so much more affecting than the loss of ice or jungle) of various Polish or Hungarian families.

As he was folding the *Wall Street Journal* in half

to make it more manageable, Mark's eye was caught by the screen on the wall of the breakfast room, permanently tuned to Bloomberg, with the sound turned down and the subtitles turned on. The word "Dunbar" was written in huge letters behind the presenter's back. What he saw not only stole his attention from the promising article about the scandal of over-regulation; it also produced the opposite emotions to the outraged complacencies he had been counting on. Unicom was making a tender offer for the common stock of the Dunbar Trust, at a very aggressive premium, which Mark quickly calculated was somewhere in the region of twenty-two percent, significantly higher than the usual offer of fifteen to twenty percent above the current market price. He immediately felt a tangle of conflicting impulses. A few minutes ago, the five hundred thousand Dunbar shares he had been given as a wedding present by his father-in-law were worth twenty-three million dollars, now they were potentially worth over twenty-eight million, but he could only realize that intoxicating five-million-dollar rush by stabbing his wife unceremoniously in the back.

How much money was enough? It was a question he found profoundly puzzling, since the money he already had gave him so little satisfaction. He seemed to fear losing it without enjoying having it. The only thing that was certain, if he was going to get away from Abby without making the rest of his life either very short or very unpleasant, was that he could not ask for any more from the Dunbars. Combined with his other assets, the twenty-eight would bring his net worth to a round fifty million. He vaguely remembered a time when that might have seemed to him a splendid sum, but the distorting influence of spending the last twenty years among billionaires now made it seem strangely inadequate.

Oh, to hell with it! It was better to live in a cottage with the woman he loved than in a palace with his ghastly wife. Farewell, Global One! Farewell, Home Lake! Farewell, estates the size of Belgium! He would run away with Mindy and live the simple life in Connecticut, or perhaps in Palm Beach (with only fifty, it really would be a simple life in that particular location) or (one crazy notion tumbling upon another) Santa Barbara? How relaxing it would be to live with Mindy by the sea, reading books he had always meant to get round to, taking trips to places he had always meant to visit, as well as returning to favorite old haunts. Life by the pool at the Cipriani wasn't so bad. "A Bellini in the hand is worth two on the wall," as his father famously said when he refused to leave that delightful watering hole in order to be dragged to some museum or church through the overcrowded streets of Venice.

One problem was that Unicom's tender offer would contain all the usual conditions about having to acquire a majority of the stock within a limited period. If he offered his stock to Unicom and they failed to complete the deal, Abby would find out and nail him to a cross for the rest of his miserable existence. It would be wiser to wait until he knew which way the wind was blowing. He had met Cogniccenti once or twice—a classic mushroom man—but it would be too risky to approach him directly. The simplest way to discover what sort of headway Unicom was making was to hurry to Abby's side in her hour of need and share her worries about Cogniccenti's outrageous act of piracy and, above all, to find out how close he was to succeeding. What bliss to be the one who threw his stock into the scales and tipped the balance, to be the man who destroyed the Dunbar Trust!

The shock that Wilson experienced when he was sacked after forty years in charge of Dunbar's legal department was trivial compared to the dismay he felt now, no longer in charge of the Trust's defenses when it was facing the launch of Unicom's hostile takeover. His earlier feelings of resentment had soon been eclipsed by his sympathy for the turmoil that his old friend was struggling with, whereas his current feeling of alarm was reinforced by that sympathy.

What could he do to help? He started to make a list of the factors that could affect the outcome, but as he wrote he realized that he could not answer the underlying question: Who was the list for? Florence and Henry were not capable of deploying it, Abigail and Megan were not fit to have it, and the legal department he had directed until recently was not allowed to share any information with him, or to consult him in any matters relating to company business. The heart of the problem was that the company had lost its leadership; everyone was an imposter compared to Dunbar, but now Dunbar had become an imposter in his own right, startled by the things he should have found most familiar and estranged from the drives that had built his empire in the first place. He had always run his emotional life like a subsidiary of the Trust, something that could be managed by negotiation and incentive, or punishment and exile. Now, it was the other way round, and all he could bring to the business was his emotional chaos. The only man who could save the company was himself in need of being saved. And yet the Board might still go with him, if he could just make himself halfway persuasive and coherent at tomorrow's meeting. His resignation of power, his strange fit of madness in London, his incarceration and his escape seemed to have brought about a revolution that might ultimately have some benefit for his soul, but in the current crisis could only be disastrous.

Wilson continued to write the list, as much to calm himself down as to explore possible tactics. There was the antitrust issue. A complaint should immediately be drawn up for the Federal Trade Commission and the Department of Justice outlining the competitive harm of letting a media company the size of Unicom take over a media company the size of Dunbar. He made a new dash on the yellow legal pad and wrote "Insider." It was an unlikely mistake, but then again there was no reason to underestimate the greed and clumsiness of people in a hurry to make money. Was there anyone close to Cogniccenti, or any shell company that had acquired Dunbar stock in anticipation of a rise in value that would inevitably follow the tender offer? That question led naturally to the next two points that he jotted down: "Creeping tender" and "Concert party." Had Unicom been covertly acquiring shares over a long period, or through third parties in order to join forces this morning?

Even as he pressed on, his confidence was undermined by not knowing his exact objective. If Dunbar and Florence were not capable of standing up for the Trust, then the only way forward would be to support Abigail and Megan's grab for power and put them in charge of defending the company's employees and assets from a hostile takeover. That was an outcome that Wilson wanted to avoid. He was fighting a battle on two fronts, while having to concede that he might have to form an alliance with one of his enemies. Normally, Wilson would have delighted in playing three-dimensional chess, but instead of enjoying the familiar sense of his own clarity and ability to think a few moves ahead of his opponents, he was suddenly engulfed by a feeling of sadness and loss.

He dropped his pen onto the pad and sank back in his armchair, staring at the dried flowers in the fireplace of his hotel suite. He thought about the first time he met Henry back in Eagle Rock, his old house in Bridle Path, where he lived with his first wife. Wilson had only been twenty-nine at the time. The senior partner who usually dealt with Dunbar was away and, in what turned out to be a misguided protection of his weekend plans, had delegated the meeting to Wilson. The maid who opened the door had led him through the house to the terrace above the sloping lawn of the garden. Dunbar was trying to organize a baseball game with his family. Abby and Megan, who were still children, were bored but compliant, while their mother, already half drunk, wearing bright yellow trousers and holding a cigarette in one hand, was making loud, mocking remarks from the edge of the improvised field. Dunbar soon spotted Wilson and the loose, disgruntled configuration formed by the game dissolved as he strode up the slope to greet his guest, but in that first glimpse Wilson had seen that Dunbar had to organize something, compete with something, and be active in some way at all times, even when he was ostensibly playing with his unwilling family on a Sunday afternoon. He had a phenomenal physical energy that made all contact with him seem urgent and adventurous.

Dunbar, who also radiated unfulfilled ambition at that time, was more impressed by what people wanted to become than by what they already were, and after spending a few hours with Wilson asked him to leave his firm and take charge of forming the legal team that would take his company public. For some reason Dunbar had immediately commanded his loyalty and inspired a level of dedication that turned out always to include Sundays. Wilson took the risk of leaving his law firm and taking an important piece of their business with him. He knew that he and Dunbar could do great things together, much greater than he could ever achieve by crawling up the hierarchy of the Toronto branch of Stone, Rucker and White.

Wilson picked up the pad and pen again. He must press on. If only Henry could regain enough focus for one last fight, maybe they could still save his life's work from the predatory Unicom.

After her torrid night with Jesus, Megan had slept until lunchtime on Wednesday. Glancing at her phone, but refusing to get involved with it just yet, she was struck by the number of missed calls she had from Abby and from just about every senior executive in the company. There were also calls from the bankers involved in Eagle Rock's acquisition of the Trust. Well, they were just going to have to wait. There was always a lot of traffic before a Board meeting, but she needed all her concentration and all her acting skills to carry off the meeting she was about to have with Kevin. She wanted Kevin to get rid of J for her. In order not to seem too capricious she would have to give him a convincing reason for liquidating his new colleague. She had settled on the fantasy that she had let slip a crucial corporate secret potentially worth hundreds of millions of dollars and that J was blackmailing her with the threat of selling the information to some rival—Unicom was the obvious choice.

Ah, here he was! She could hear the doorbell ringing and prepared an agitated, deeply preoccupied and tragic look to greet him with.

———

Dunbar knew exactly where he was: he was in the dining room of Florence's apartment in New York, drinking a small cup of coffee after lunch. Florence was talking to Wilson on the phone, his old friend Wilson, to whom he owed an apology for his unfair sacking. Everything in the room looked bright and a little startling as the light flooded in through the glass doors of the surrounding terrace. He had come close to insanity and to death; he had been beside himself with anxiety that he might not see Florence before he died, and yet here he was staying in her apartment. Far from the mediocrity of returning to normal, things were better than they had ever been. For the first time in weeks he felt that his body was made of one substance, rather than held together, like a favorite old toy, with rags and tape and string. He had slept and eaten and the bad meds forced on him by Dr. Bob and Dr. Harris seemed to have been purged by his Cumbrian ordeal and to have lost their hold over his mind and mood. He had always taken a certain physical solidity for granted and only noticed it when it was taken away. Just for the moment he was as surprised to have it back as he had been to lose it. It was familiar and strange in equal measure, like the first hour of arriving at Home Lake at the beginning of the summer when a thousand forgotten details rushed back and insisted that they had been there all along.

He struggled to define what it was he was feeling underneath that tangle of novelty and recognition.

There was some ground to it all, something he had scarcely ever known, except maybe when Catherine agreed to marry him, but then it had been much more euphoric than this steady and fundamental sense of something. Perhaps it was gratitude; perhaps that was the right name for the ground he was now standing on. Yes, he felt—his vocabulary was venturing into new territory here—blessed. It was out of character for him to care about identifying his feelings beyond the basic division between the ones he liked and the ones he didn't. He had never had much of a language for exploring his motivation, or any motive to develop one. He had always been lost in action, driven by what he had taken to be the self-evident truth that there could be nothing more meaningful than accumulating power and money. It was late to be beginning an introspective journey, but he knew he had no choice. The last few weeks had not just been about madness; they had taken him away from the world of facts and statistics and laws into a world of metaphors and insights and obscure connections. He was not flying out of a war zone he need never return to; he was still in a maze that he couldn't get out of except by going through its center. Nevertheless, he felt he was near its center and that he might be able to find his way out, given time.

"Hello, Daddy," said Florence, coming back into the dining room.

"Darling!" said Dunbar, "I was just thinking how happy, well, how blessed I feel."

Florence rested both hands on his shoulders and

leant over to kiss the top of his head. "I don't think I've ever heard you use that word before."

"Yes," said Dunbar, "it's a first." He smiled at her, a little embarrassed.

She pressed gently on his shoulders to reassure him.

"Wilson would like to come over at five o'clock to discuss a few things with you, if that's all right."

"Yes, yes," said Dunbar, falling over himself trying to catch up with his guilt, "I must apologize more fully. I thanked him this morning and gave him his job back."

"He's never really stopped doing it," said Florence, "but I know he's happy to have your confidence back."

"I'd like to have my confidence back as well," said Dunbar.

"It's so great that it *is* coming back," said Florence. "I was thinking we might go for a walk in the Park, if you'd like that. It's such a beautiful day and Wilson won't be here for a couple of hours."

"Yes, I'd love that," said Dunbar.

As the two of them rode down together in the elevator, Dunbar noticed that he felt a kind of inexplicable pleasure in everything. Danny, the elevator man, who Florence had greeted when they got in, seemed to be a person of almost saintly beneficence; the triangular brown button leather seat in the corner of the elevator had the curious charm and intensity of the miniature; the dark gray and gold hall glowed with mirrors and flowers. The doorman was obviously in love with Florence, and who could blame him? In fact, the whole experience reminded Dunbar of *A Day in the Park*, one of the favorite books of his early childhood, in which Bobby, a boy in shorts and a yellow sweater, goes with his elegant mother, who is wearing a cream-colored pleated dress and a pair of dark glasses, to buy a balloon in Central Park. The story had almost no point at all and yet it exerted a fascination on him when he was four that was close to the feeling of gratuitous delight that he was having right now, crossing Fifth Avenue toward the Park's nearest entrance, with Florence by his side.

Asked which way he wanted to go, Dunbar chose the path that curved down to the Conservatory Pond, where people went to sail model boats on the water.

"I've been thinking about our talk on the plane last night," he said. "I feel much more rested now and . . ."

"Blessed?" said Florence, smiling.

"I knew I was going to be teased about that word," said Dunbar, smiling back at her. "I was going to say 'solid,' but it sounded a bit odd. The point is I'd like to take up your offer and come with you to Wyoming."

"That's wonderful," said Florence.

"At least for a few weeks, or maybe longer."

"As long as you like."

"Your sisters don't know this yet, and technically it has to go through the directors, but Wilson persuaded me to buy back the Trust's property assets and I've put in a strong offer. They're not part of the core business, just good investments, land on the edge of Vancouver and Toronto and other big cities, worth near enough a billion. All that'll go to you and your kids, along with the art and the houses . . ."

"I think we've got enough already," said Florence, hesitating a little, so as to make it clear that she was touched by his intention. "Why don't we make a foundation? Buy some land and *not* build on it."

"You certainly know how to provoke an old capitalist," said Dunbar.

"It's a fair trade," said Florence: "for every acre you develop, buy a hundred acres and leave them just as they are."

"I'll think about it," said Dunbar, already knowing he would agree. "Just being useless," he added.

"Useless to us," said Florence.

"Yes," said Dunbar, "I understand," he trailed off. "Your sisters," he said, anchoring himself back in more established ground, "have a lust for power, and I can't pretend I don't know where it comes from, but right now I don't see any reason not to let them have what they want. The Dunbar Trust will still be one of the greatest companies in the world, whoever runs it. That'll be my legacy . . ."

Dunbar stopped. There was a look of excruciating pain on Florence's face as she pressed her hand against the side of her neck.

"What's wrong?" he asked, reaching out to hold her arm.

"I'm sorry. I just suddenly felt this sharp pain in my neck. It was like a bee sting, but the bees can't be awake at this time of year."

"Let me have a look; you never know with these crazy seasons."

Florence unclasped her hand.

"There's a little trickle of blood," said Dunbar.

"It's probably some kid with a BB gun," said Florence, sounding unconcerned but looking pale and upset.

"We must get a doctor to have a look at it," said Dunbar, his heart pounding violently and his ears suddenly deafened by internal ringing.

"Oh, there's no need for a doctor," said Florence, "I'll just put some disinfectant on it and have a rest while you're talking to Wilson."

"Let's go back in," said Dunbar, no longer feeling as solid as he had claimed to be only a few minutes before.

Abby had decided, without having the time to look into the matter thoroughly, that she was having the worst day of her life. She had been on the phone hour after hour talking to the senior management of the Trust and to the directors who were due at the Board meeting at ten o'clock the next morning. In the midst of this extraordinary crisis, Meg had failed to answer her phone until three o'clock and was then amazed to hear the news, which everyone else had been talking about nonstop since the moment it came on the wire just before the opening of the stock market. When they finally spoke, Abby found it hard to believe that Meg had no idea about Unicom, and she even entertained the suspicion that Meg might have sold her shares to Cogniccenti at the high premium he was offering. It would be an insane thing to do, but then Meg was capable of almost anything.

She and Meg each had fifteen percent of the Trust's stock (the ten they had originally received and the half of Florence's share they had each been given when she turned her back on the company) and they only had to get just over twenty percent more to block the majority that was needed for a merger to be forced on the company. Still, it was maddening to be thinking of defensive actions when they had been quietly planning to take the company private the next day, at what now turned out to be a considerably lower price than Unicom was offering the shareholders. She was beginning to think that it might be more skillful to present Eagle Rock's privatization of the company as a white knight that just happened to be on hand, fully armed and ready to buy the company in order to save it, but any attempt to present Eagle Rock's bid as a contingency plan that had been in place for a long time, ready to deal with just such an emergency, was impossible in view of the second-worst piece of news she had heard that day: Dunbar had reinstated Wilson as his counsel and they were both attending tomorrow's Board meeting.

The most fundamental problem, however, was money. She and Bild would have to raise more debt. Eagle Rock already had big lines of credit with JP Morgan, Citibank, and Morgan Stanley, but they might have to start selling off some non-core assets to raise the money to buy the rest of the company. It was all getting crushingly complicated. Why hadn't Bild returned her endless calls? He was the only one who could work out what to do and make it happen.

Dunbar thanked Wilson one more time as the doors of the elevator closed in the hall of Florence's apartment. His apology to Wilson had been as effortless and natural as Wilson's dismissal of any grievances. During their meeting over the last three hours, Wilson had persuaded Dunbar to go into battle one more time. The news of Unicom's tender offer and the rumors coming from some of the directors, whose loyalty to Dunbar and Wilson exceeded their discretion, that Abby and Megan were trying to take the company private, convinced Dunbar to postpone the announcement of his complete retirement.

He was eager to see Florence, who had been resting since their walk in the Park. He knew there was something radically different about his attitude toward tomorrow's battle, something about himself that he didn't recognize. The idea of the Trust that bore his name being devoured by Unicom was theoretically repulsive to him, as was the prospect of his two older daughters privatizing the company by incurring massive debt, sacking thousands of employees, and spinning off some of its less profitable, but most influential and visible holdings. Nevertheless, there had been something missing in his response to this calamitous news. He puzzled over what had happened and then suddenly realized that he wasn't feeling furious. Like

a familiar painting that only gets noticed because it
has been removed, leaving a bare hook and silhouette
of dirt on the wall, only the absence of his fury could
make him see just how much of his famous "energy"
used to be derived from a more or less perpetual argument with the unsatisfactory nature of things, briefly
appeased by the occasional big victory, but always renewed by a boundless sense of frustration. His reconciliation with Florence seemed to have given him a
sense of peace that was too deep for a corporate war,
even such a personal one, to disturb. He and Wilson
would go in tomorrow and try to get control out of the
hands of his greedy and selfish daughters and give it
to his two most trusted senior executives; they would
say their piece and join forces one last time to try to
save the company, but he would leave the results to
the directors and to fate and, whatever happened, he
would head out with Florence tomorrow for a life of
family and philanthropy. He had been recast in some
furnace that he had neither sought nor devised and
now he seemed to have no fury or ambition left, only
love. Dunbar reached out his hand and leant against
the wall to support himself, his breath catching in his
throat as he took in the magnitude of what had happened to him and the thought that he might have died
without experiencing it.

17

Despite his exhaustion, Dr. Bob's anxiety had robbed him of sleep. With a groan and a curse, he threw aside the bedclothes and swung his legs to the floor. It was only five o'clock, but he might as well get up. This was going to be one of the most fraught and crucial days of his life. He just needed to get to the end of it. Between Cogniccenti and the Dunbar girls, he had enough money to retire and become his own personal physician, the sole recipient of his extravagant prescriptions and his expert care, but he needed to walk away without Abby and Megan knowing for sure that he had betrayed them and without Cogniccenti's chilling disappointment at his failure to get rid of Dunbar having any occasion to grow stronger. He had taken the precaution of buying a ticket for the nine o'clock flight to Zurich that evening. But right now he needed to be sharp. He shook a couple of thirty-milligram Adderall into his palm and washed them down with the water on his bedside table. Then, reflecting on how ineffective they had become recently, he took a third.

"What the fuck, Dick? You didn't answer my calls all day yesterday and now you call me at six-thirty in the morning."

"Abby," said Dick Bild, "I sincerely apologize, but yesterday was the worst ambush of my career. Unicom was a grenade in the swimming pool. We were carrying people out on stretchers; I saw some of the toughest traders in the business with tears in their eyes. I had the whole office focused on the single purpose of acquiring the extra twenty percent of the stock that would get Eagle Rock across the line and at least block the Unicom merger. We were supposed to be hitting a home run today. And now we can only succeed by building a second tower of debt next to the one we've already built."

"You should have secured the shares earlier," said Abby bitterly.

"Don't lecture me on my business," said Dick, with a touch of menace. "If you start a buyout too early it drives the price up, and you end up with every arbitrage vulture in London and New York tearing the heart out of your profits. Anyhow, we had five of the best brokerage houses buying the stock gradually on our behalf. We were supposed to have it all locked down by the middle of your Board meeting, but yesterday one fucking house after another was saying it didn't have the stock ready yet, or that it hadn't been able to acquire enough of it. I think the fuckers sold it to Cogniccenti. Some asshole must have told him where to go shopping."

"Someone in your organization?"

"Abby, like I said, the office was full of grown men in tears: they were crying over their Christmas bonuses. We've put three months of work into this Eagle Rock deal. Everyone in the office is one hundred percent committed."

"This is a king-sized fuck-up," said Abby.

"Calm down," said Dick. "We still have options. We can keep on trying to get all the scraps we can, and we can run a counter-ad, appealing to the loyalty of the old Dunbar shareholders. The brokerage firms had a lot of shares, but a lot more are still out there in Shareholder Land, in the hands of millions of ordinary people. The trouble is we'll have to renegotiate our credit to make a better offer than Unicom."

"Well, get on it," said Abby.

"I'm on it."

Dunbar was reluctant to knock on Florence's door, in case she was still asleep. When he had dropped in on her after saying good-bye to Wilson, she had apologized and said that she was feeling a little nauseous and would rather stay in bed. Resting her hands on her abdomen, she said that she was having cramps, which he tactfully assumed meant she was getting her period and that he should ask no further questions.

She had said she wanted to get a good night's sleep since there was so much going on the next day.

There was still time to let her rest a little longer. She wasn't even going to the meeting, after all, and Wilson wasn't picking him up for an hour or so. In the meantime he would busy himself getting ready. He spread out his white shirt and dark gray suit, his maroon tie with a subtle diamond pattern of its own color, and his gold cufflinks: the sort of clothes he had worn for decades but which now felt strange and slightly comical.

As he stood under the shower a few minutes later, it seemed enough to let the water, like rain on a hillside, form its own streams as it ran down his body. It seemed enough to do nothing. He was feeling a kind of unprecedented calm. Unicom might devour the company, his daughters might take it private, and it might remain intact and be run by its loyal senior management; just for the moment he was at ease with all the possible outcomes. He felt that this resignation to fate was at once hidden and obvious, like the tears that he could feel stinging the corners of his eyes but that were invisible among the streams of water rushing over his face. He was crying out of gratitude, and he was grateful to be crying. He didn't even care if he became the kind of foolish old man who cried all the time; it was such a relief to stop trying to control himself anymore. He had imagined that his life's work was to build one of the most powerful organizations in the world, but now he felt that it had all really been leading to the rehabilitation of his innocence. It was a seemingly circular journey that had forced him to crawl through a second childhood, but had then unexpectedly continued backward, through his Cumbrian ordeal, to something more like a second birth. An apparently circular pattern had opened up at the last moment into a new realm in which everything seemed to be perfect just as it was.

Some residual practicality eventually allowed Dunbar to turn off the shower, step out, and wrap himself in a towel. Walking slowly back into the bedroom, he glanced at the clothes on the bed but was unable to take seriously the idea that he should start getting dressed. Instead, he subsided into the armchair in the corner of the room, between the window and the chest of drawers, astonished, at his age, to be experiencing something for the first time.

There was a knock on the door and, before he had time to answer it, Florence came into his room in her dressing gown, walked unsteadily over to the bed, and sank down onto the mattress. Her face was astonishingly pale and she was clearly struggling to master her physical state.

"I'm sorry, Daddy," she said, with some difficulty, "I wouldn't normally barge in on you like this, but I've been feeling really terrible. I don't know what's wrong; I've been vomiting. In fact, I'm going to have to move into one of the children's rooms; mine needs clearing up. I couldn't control it. It's not really fair on . . ."

Florence broke short her sentence and leant forward over her folded arms, groaning with pain.

"Jesus," said Dunbar, sitting down next to her and putting his arm across her stooped back. "We must call a doctor." He clasped her shoulder, as much to reassure himself as Florence.

"I've already called him," she gasped. "Do you mind letting him in?"

"Of course not," said Dunbar.

"Oh, God," said Florence, lurching forward and retching.

"My darling," said Dunbar. "What's going on?"

"I don't know . . ."

"Lie here, lie here, I'll get a bowl," said Dunbar.

He got up, his heart beating wildly. As he looked down he saw with horror that the mess on the carpet was red with blood. He reeled from the room, feeling a wave of wild panic and passionate opposition—if there was a God and he let Florence come to any serious harm, he was no better than a criminal lunatic.

Where was the doctor? Where was the bloody doctor?

Kevin had invited himself to breakfast to "go over some security issues" and it was logical to assume that he was the person ringing the doorbell, but J was busy preparing his muscle-building, energy-boosting patent smoothie, and it would have taken four strong men to stop him from setting those rotary blades in motion. He also took the time to switch on the kettle before ambling over to the front door of his studio flat

and welcoming Kevin, over the whine of the blender
and the incipient rumble of the heating water, into its
plain interior. Only one object decorated the white
walls of the room: a gently curved black samurai
sword resting on almost invisible nails over the pallet
bed on the far side of the room.

"Wotcha, mate!" said Kevin, with a geniality that
immediately made J suspicious. He was clearly about
to make some unpleasant request, or deliver some
harsh news.

"How's it going?" said J, returning to the kitchen
counter and switching off the blender at the very moment that the kettle reached its shuddering climax
and clicked itself off. J savored the faultless efficiency
and effortless synergy. Ever since he had been with
Megan, everything was just flowing so beautifully. It
was like perfect sex, or like perfect intuition, when
you could shoot through a partition at the exact right
point and hear the body fall on the other side.

He didn't much care what that sour old fuck Kevin
had come to complain about; tomorrow he would be
flying to Maui on a private jet with Megan and catching mangos as they fell from the trees. As he savored
his feeling of superiority, as well as the no less delicious prospect of the giant energy boost he was about
to get from combining a pint of fresh black coffee with
a pint of pale green protein, a slight change of light on
the bulging stainless steel surface of the kettle caught
his attention. He could see a strangely enlarged reflection of Kevin's hand reaching inside his brown leather

coat, and with that battle alertness he had just been reflecting on, he knew that Kevin was reaching for a weapon.

Spinning round, he swung the kettle upward through the air, splashing Kevin in a ribbon of boiling water from his wrist to his face, and at the same time kicking him between the legs as hard as possible. As Kevin lurched forward, J brought the kettle down on the crown of his head, grabbed his right arm, and twisted it until the gun fell from his hand. He kicked the pistol across the floor to the corner of the room and, after punching Kevin in the side of the head, walked over to the bed and took the curved black sword from its hanging place on the wall.

Kevin, to give him his due, was a warrior and despite severe burns, partial blinding, and two disabling blows, was back on his feet and had managed to grab a knife from the magnetic strip above the cooker. J threw aside the scabbard of the sword and walked toward his opponent with the blade drawn back and ready to strike.

"Man, I knew you were jealous," said J, "but I didn't know you were crazy."

"Jealous?" Kevin said, sucking in his pain. "She's the one who fucking sent me here."

"Take back that dirty lie," said J.

"It's true, mate. She said you were blackmailing her and that she wanted you dead."

"No," shouted J. "No!"

Even as he tried to deny it, J knew that Kevin was

telling the truth. The only thing he could trust in this world of shit was the weapon he was holding in his hands.

"No!" he shouted, one more time, slicing through Kevin's neck.

J cleaned the blade of his sword with a tea cloth folded neatly by the sink. As he slid the sword back into its scabbard, he emptied his mind of every thought except revenge.

"You should go to your meeting," said Florence.

"I'm not leaving you," said Dunbar. "Wilson can go to the meeting for me."

"I'm not leaving either of you until we know what's going on," said Wilson.

"We've got an ambulance that is currently six minutes away," said the doctor.

"Oh, stop being so loyal, both of you," said Florence, but even as she tried to sound carefree and practical, she was forced to turn away again and vomit into a bowl already full of blood and bile. "Apart from anything else," she added, "I don't want anyone to see me in this state."

"Can I stay, at least?" said Chris, who was sitting on the edge of the bed, with his hand resting on the outline of her leg. "You forget," he said, smiling, "we went round Mexico together twice, I'm used to seeing you like this."

"This is different," said Florence, showing her fear

for the first time, "It's as if I'm vomiting myself. I've never felt this sick before."

When she saw the expression on her father's face, Florence immediately regretted giving in to the relief of talking directly to Chris.

"For God's sake," shouted Dunbar to the doctor, as if he might relent under enough emotional pressure and reveal that he had a solution after all. "Can't you do something?"

"This is not an average house call," said the doctor drily. "When the ambulance arrives we're going to administer a powerful antiemetic, get started on an activated charcoal lavage, and send the blood sample and the skin sample from the puncture wound to the emergency pathology lab. She'll be in the intensive care unit of the Presbyterian Hospital within half an hour, getting some of the best medical treatment available anywhere in the world. It would be helpful to the patient if we could all stay calm."

Dunbar stared at the doctor dumbly.

"Intensive care unit," he repeated in a hoarse whisper.

Megan sat in the back of her car, vaguely waiting for Abby to come out of her building, and urgently waiting for a text from Kevin. They had agreed on a code. An hour after his breakfast meeting with J, she had texted an innocent request for him to meet her at the Dunbar Building after the Board meeting. If he had successfully dealt with J, he would reply, "Understood"; if there was some kind of problem or delay he would reply, "I'll be there." Instead, there was no reply at all.

She refused to worry, she simply refused to, but her anxiety, unlike so many of the employees in her compliant entourage, refused her refusal and took control of her imagination. What if Kevin and Jesus had agreed to collaborate in some way? They were brothers in arms, after all. Who knew what weird bonds developed among men who had been officially sanctioned to maim, kill, and torture? What if J had prevailed? Would she be able to persuade him that Kevin had been acting out of insane jealousy and that she was going to light a thousand candles to thank God for sparing J's precious life?

"Hi," said Abby, startling Megan out of her thoughts. "What a dreadful fucking day . . ."

"Oh, hi, it's great to see you, too," said Meg, grabbing at sarcasm to stop herself from drowning in the torrent of questions that had been sweeping her away before her sister's arrival.

"I'm sorry," said Abby, "but I've had such an annoying conversation with Dick Bild this morning. He's totally screwed up. He hasn't been able to secure the shares we had lined up. We're going to have to borrow more money, which will eat into our profits . . ."

"We might as well not go to the fucking meeting at all," said Megan, alarmed by her sudden indifference to making money, compared to her terror of being imprisoned.

"For God's sake, Meg," Abby began, but a glance at her sister's clenched profile silenced her. She had hardly ever seen Megan frightened and she had never seen her in despair; now both emotions were combined in a single rigid stare. She transferred her exasperation to the driver.

"What are you waiting for? Let's go."

"This should be fun," said Cogniccenti, switching on his computer. "I've set up a connection with a new member of the Board, whose anonymity I'll protect by simply calling him 'Dr. Bob.'"

"That asshole," said Dick Bild, "what the fuck is he doing on the Board?"

"The girls have put him there as a reward for certain favors."

"Percocet Extra Strength favors, or Dunbar Trust favors?"

"I imagine the prescriptions flowed pretty freely, but he also played a key part in Dunbar's fall from power."

"Not key enough," said Bild. "I hear the old man arrived back in the city last night. Even Victor used to avoid locking antlers with Henry Dunbar. I guess that's why we're listening in. See if he's still got the old mojo."

"Mojo?" said Cogniccenti. "The guy was certifiably insane until two days ago. Without you the Eagle Rock bid is already dead in the water. What's he going to do, make a stirring speech explaining to the Board that it's their fiduciary responsibility to turn down a twenty-two percent premium so they can spend the rest of their lives being sued by angry shareholders?"

Steve put a couple of bottles of cold Japanese beer on the table; as if the two men were settling down to watch a football game.

"It's a done deal, Dick," said Steve, leaning forward to raise the volume on his computer: "just enjoy the show."

18

"No," said Dunbar. "Not Florence."

"I'm sorry," said the doctor, more stunned than usual by the inadequacy of his words.

"We must give her new organs," said Dunbar, "put her on some machines while they're being replaced. Take mine, if you can't get others soon enough. I know they're old, but they still work."

Dunbar peeled off his jacket and slipped the tie from his neck.

"Mr. Dunbar . . ." the doctor began.

"It's not natural for her to die first," said Dunbar, unbuttoning his collar. "It should be the other way round. Take anything she needs: heart, lungs, liver, kidneys, eyes, whatever might save her life."

"Mr. Dunbar, there's nothing we can do," said the doctor, putting a restraining hand on Dunbar's arm. "I'm sorry. The whole body is septic, the new organs would just start to fail as soon as we put them in."

Florence had been poisoned with Abrin, a toxin for which there was no antidote, combined in this case with other poisons to make her death more certain and more painful. Her system was being purged and her blood changed, which would give her a little more time, but her body was already caught up in an irreversible process of collapse.

Dunbar continued to unbutton his shirt until it was open to the waist.

"What are you doing?" asked Florence, waking from the heavy sedation she was under.

"I want to donate . . ."

"Oh, Daddy," said Florence, her eyes filling with tears.

Dunbar reached out and clasped Florence's hand. With a mixture of relief and dread, he realized that he could not feel the anesthetic numbness that had spread over him when he was told that Catherine was not going to "make it." There were no battlements left around his heart to postpone his surrender to sorrow and desolation. Was this the triumph of self-knowledge: to suffer more lucidly? And yet he had felt blessed for the first time only the day before. There was something obscene about the indiscriminate clarity of his new mind. If only he had gone with Florence to Wyoming, if only he had renounced his power a little sooner. Now he was like a man whose sight has been restored just in time to be wheeled in front of *The Flaying of Marsyas*, unable to move, unable to leave, knowing he will never see the other galleries again.

"We'll be right outside," said the doctor to Florence, "just press this button if you need any help."

Florence nodded, but said nothing, as if she only had a certain number of words left and meant to use them carefully. Once the doctor and the nurses had left the room, she managed to speak again.

"It's not that I'm frightened of dying," she said. "It's more that I'm upset about the other people it will hurt . . . and the waste of love."

She glanced over to Chris for a moment, as if to ask for his forgiveness on behalf of all the people who would be hurt by her death.

"The waste of love," repeated Dunbar, shattered by his daughter's verdict and by the landscape it forced him to imagine.

"Oh, Daddy," said Florence, speaking in an emphatic whisper, "I'm so glad we reconciled before it was too late."

"But it is too late," said Dunbar, unable to stop himself.

"I know . . ." she said. "The children—I can't bear to let them down when they're so young."

Dunbar struggled to find an exonerating formula for his tormented daughter, but the effort of speaking proved too much for her and before he could relieve Florence of her blameless guilt, she closed her eyes again and lay motionless on the bed, barely breathing.

"She's resting," said Wilson, "let's sit down for a while."

Dunbar seemed to crumble as he sank into one of the armchairs in the corner of his daughter's room.

Above the formality of his polished black shoes and charcoal trousers, his abdomen and his chest were exposed in an incongruous streak of nakedness. He watched the tufts of white hair rise and fall with his breathing, as if he were observing someone else's body for signs of life.

"No mercy," said Dunbar, pressing his hands to his head, "in this world, or any other."

He felt pain gripping his forehead like a metal band. Soon, a second belt of pain started tightening around his chest. He crossed his arms and clasped his sides, as if hugging himself after a long separation, and then slouched back into the chair, struggling to breathe. He felt the onset of that boundless dread, the untethered astronaut tumbling through the stale darkness of space. And then he felt a heavy flood in his head, like the time he flipped backward and cracked his skull on the path in Davos; he had seemed to be suspended on the thick threshold of passing out, registering the emergency with a strange detachment, his head flooding with a foretaste of oblivion.

Before he knew what was going on, the doctor was by his side, calling out instructions to the nurses. Dunbar heard the words "defibrillator" and "oxygen" and felt the atmosphere of alarm closing around him like the pain clutching at his head and heart.

"Don't worry, Mr. Dunbar," said the doctor, who was already holding a syringe at the ready. "We're going to get rid of that pain right away."

"Please don't," gasped Dunbar. "I've had enough; I've seen enough."

"I know you're very distressed at this moment . . ."

"What is it you don't want me to miss?" said Dunbar. "Watching my daughter die in front of me?"

"And how is it you want her to spend the last few hours of her life," the doctor replied: "watching you die in front of her?"

Dunbar recognized the truth of what the doctor had said, and resignedly held out his arm for the injection. He must stand by Florence as she died and pour whatever was left of his vitality and kindness into her, holding back his own annihilation.

"More life," he muttered, as the clear liquid joined his bloodstream and dissolved the tension in his head and chest. "Do you mind if I have a word alone with Wilson and Chris?"

"Of course not," said the doctor politely, as if there had never been a moment's discord between them.

"Charlie," said Dunbar, leaning forward to talk more privately to his friend. "I don't want to talk about . . . I can't talk about . . ."

"I understand," said Wilson.

"But when this is over, can you stop these bastards from saving my life?"

"We could draw up a living will for you."

"Make it happen," said Dunbar, as if trying to remember a quotation. "Don't let the girls get hold of the company. Help Cogniccenti, if that's the only way to keep them from getting control. And find out if either of them was involved in poisoning Florence and, if so, then make sure that she spends the rest of her life in prison."

"I'll make sure of it," said Wilson. "Abby's already wanted by the British police in connection with Peter Walker's suicide."

Dunbar sank back in the chair a second time.

"He committed suicide?" he said.

"I'm sorry, I thought Florence had told you."

"No," said Dunbar, staring across the room, temporarily emptied by the surfeit of horror, as if there was no room left for thought or speech, or any specific grief. He could see Florence lying motionless on the bed, with her eyes shut. Chris sat beside her, watching her breathe.

"No, she didn't tell me," said Dunbar eventually. "Poor Peter, he was my friend. I couldn't have made it without him."

He looked at Wilson with passionate disbelief.

"How has it come to this, Charlie? Why is your son watching my daughter die? Why has everything been destroyed, just as I've started to understand it for the first time?"

"All of us will be blown to dust," said Wilson, "but the understanding won't be destroyed and it can't be, as long as someone is left standing who still prefers to tell the truth."

Acknowledgments

I want to thank my friend Dominic Armstrong for his expert collaboration in writing about the business and financial aspects of this story.

I am also grateful to John Rogerson for his help with some of the legal questions brought up by the plot of this novel.

I want to thank Monica Carmona for drawing my attention to the Hogarth Shakespeare series and Juliet Brooke for her excellent editing once I was invited to be a part of it.

I would also like to thank Jane Longman and Francis Wyndham for continuing to be my first and most encouraging readers.

ABOUT THE AUTHOR

Edward St. Aubyn was born in London. His superbly acclaimed Patrick Melrose novels are *Never Mind*, which won a Betty Trask Award; *Bad News*; *Some Hope*; *Mother's Milk*, which won the Prix Femina étranger and was shortlisted for the Man Booker Prize; and *At Last*. He is also the author of the novels *A Clue to the Exit*; *On the Edge*, which was short-listed for the Guardian Fiction Prize; and *Lost for Words*, which won the Bollinger Everyman Wodehouse Prize.

Hogarth Shakespeare

For more than four hundred years, Shakespeare's works have been performed, read, and loved throughout the world. They have been reinterpreted for each new generation, whether as teen films, musicals, science-fiction flicks, Japanese warrior tales, or literary transformations.

The Hogarth Press was founded by Virginia and Leonard Woolf in 1917 with a mission to publish the best new writing of the age. In 2012, Hogarth was launched in London and New York to continue the tradition. The Hogarth Shakespeare project sees Shakespeare's works retold by acclaimed and bestselling novelists of today. The series launched in October 2015 and to date will be published in twenty countries.

THE TEMPEST
retold by
MARGARET ATWOOD

OTHELLO
retold by
TRACY CHEVALIER

HAMLET
retold by
GILLIAN FLYNN

THE MERCHANT OF VENICE
retold by
HOWARD JACOBSON

MACBETH
retold by
JO NESBØ

KING LEAR
retold by
EDWARD ST. AUBYN

THE TAMING OF THE SHREW
retold by
ANNE TYLER

THE WINTER'S TALE
retold by
JEANETTE WINTERSON